WHAT DO FISH HAVE TO DO WITH ANYTHING?

AND OTHER STORIES

WHAT DO FISH HAVE TO DO WITH ANYTHING?

AND OTHER STORIES

illustrated by
Tracy Mitchell

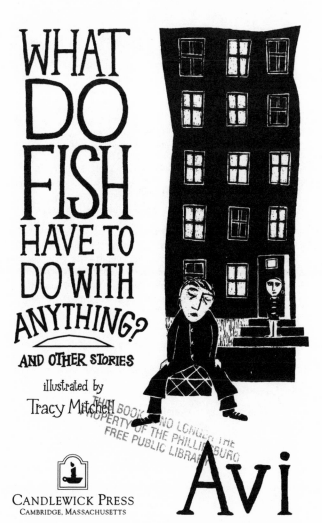

Avi

CANDLEWICK PRESS
CAMBRIDGE, MASSACHUSETTS

For Billy

Text copyright © 1997 by Avi
Illustrations copyright © 1997 by Tracy Mitchell

All rights reserved.

First edition 1997

Library of Congress Cataloging-in-Publication Data

Avi, date.
What do fish have to do with anything? : short stories / by Avi. — 1st ed.
Contents: What do fish have to do with anything? — The goodness of Matt
Kaizer — Talk to me — Teacher tamer — Pets — What's inside — Fortune cookie.
ISBN 0-7636-0329-5 (hardcover) — ISBN 0-7636-0412-7 (paperback)
1. Children's stories, American. [1. Short stories.] I. Title.
PZ7. A953Wf   1997
[Fic] — dc21   97-1354

2 4 6 8 10 9 7 5 3 1

Printed in the United States of America

This book was typeset in Slimbach.

Candlewick Press
2067 Massachusetts Avenue
Cambridge, Massachusetts 02140

Also by Avi:

Blue Heron
City of Light, City of Dark
Devil's Race
Nothing but the Truth
A Place Called Ugly
Sometimes I Think I Hear My Name
Wolf Rider

CONTENTS

9

WHAT DO FISH HAVE TO DO WITH ANYTHING?

35

THE GOODNESS OF MATT KAIZER

61

TALK TO ME

93

TEACHER TAMER

121

PETS

153

WHAT'S INSIDE

175

FORTUNE COOKIE

WHAT DO FISH HAVE TO DO WITH ANYTHING?

Every day at three o'clock Mrs. Markham waited for her son, Willie, to come out of school. They walked home together. If asked why she did it, Mrs. Markham would say, "Parents need to watch their children."

As they left the schoolyard, Mrs. Markham inevitably asked, "How was school?"

Willie would begin to talk, then stop. He was never sure his mother was listening. She seemed preoccupied with her own thoughts. She had been like that ever since his dad had abandoned them six months ago. No one knew where he'd gone. Willie had the feeling that his mother was lost too. It made him feel lonely.

One Monday afternoon, as they approached the apartment building where they lived, she suddenly tugged at him. "Don't look that way," she said.

"Where?"

"At that man over there."

Willie stole a look over his shoulder. A man, whom Willie had never seen before, was sitting on a red plastic milk crate near the curb. His matted, streaky gray hair hung like a ragged curtain over his dirty face. His shoes were torn. Rough hands lay upon his knees. One hand was palm up. No one seemed to pay him any mind. Willie was certain he had never seen a man so utterly alone. It was as if he were some spat-out piece of chewing gum on the pavement.

"What's the matter with him?" Willie asked his mother in a hushed voice.

Keeping her eyes straight ahead, Mrs. Markham

said, "He's sick." She pulled Willie around. "Don't stare. It's rude."

"What kind of sick?"

As Mrs. Markham searched for an answer, she began to walk faster. "He's unhappy," she said.

"What's he doing?"

"Come on, Willie, you know perfectly well. He's begging."

"Do you think anyone gave him anything?"

"I don't know. Now, come on, don't look."

"Why don't you give him anything?"

"We have nothing to spare."

When they got home, Mrs. Markham removed a white cardboard box from the refrigerator. It contained pound cake. Using her thumb as a measure, she carefully cut a half-inch piece of cake and gave it to Willie on a clean plate. The plate lay on a plastic mat decorated with images of roses with diamondlike dewdrops. She also gave him a glass of milk and a folded napkin. She moved slowly.

Willie said, "Can I have a bigger piece of cake?"

Mrs. Markham picked up the cake box and ran a manicured pink fingernail along the nutrition information panel. "A half-inch piece is a portion, and a portion contains the following health requirements. Do you want to hear them?"

"No."

"It's on the box, so you can believe what it says. Scientists study people, then write these things. If you're smart enough you could become a scientist. Like this." Mrs. Markham tapped the box. "It pays well."

Willie ate his cake and drank the milk. When he was done he took care to wipe the crumbs off his face as well as to blot his milk mustache with the napkin. His mother liked him to be neat.

His mother said, "Now go on and do your homework. Carefully. You're in sixth grade. It's important."

Willie gathered up his books that lay on the empty third chair. At the kitchen entrance he paused and looked back at his mother. She was staring sadly at the cake box, but he didn't think she was seeing it. Her unhappiness made him think of the man on the street.

"What *kind* of unhappiness do you think he has?" he suddenly asked.

"Who's that?"

"That man."

Mrs. Markham looked puzzled.

"The begging man. The one on the street."

"Oh, could be anything," his mother said, vaguely. "A person can be unhappy for many reasons." She turned to stare out the window, as if an answer might be there.

"Is unhappiness a sickness you can cure?"

"I wish you wouldn't ask such questions."

"Why?"

After a moment she said, "Questions that have no answers shouldn't be asked."

"Can I go out?"

"Homework first."

Willie turned to go again.

"Money," Mrs. Markham suddenly said. "Money will cure a lot of unhappiness. That's why that man was begging. A salesman once said to me, 'Maybe you can't buy happiness, but you can rent a lot of it.' You should remember that."

"How much money do we have?"

"Not enough."

"Is that why you're unhappy?"

"Willie, do your homework."

Willie started to ask another question, but decided he would not get an answer. He left the kitchen.

The apartment had three rooms. The walls were painted mint green. Willie walked down the hallway to his room, which was at the front of the building. By climbing up on the windowsill and pressing against the glass he could see the sidewalk five stories below. The man was still there.

It was almost five when he went to tell his mother he had finished his school assignments. He found her in her dim bedroom, sleeping. Since she had begun working the night shift at a convenience store—two weeks now—she took naps in the late afternoon.

For a while Willie stood on the threshold, hoping his mother would wake up. When she didn't, he went to the front room and looked down on the street again. The begging man had not moved.

Willie returned to his mother's room.

"I'm going out," he announced—softly.

Willie waited a decent interval for his mother to waken. When she did not, he made sure his keys were in his pocket. Then he left the apartment.

By standing just outside the building door, he could keep his eyes on the man. It appeared as if he had still not moved. Willie wondered how anyone could go without moving for so long in the chill October air. Was staying still part of the man's sickness?

During the twenty minutes that Willie watched, no one who passed looked in the beggar's direction. Willie wondered if they even saw the man. Certainly no one put any money into his open hand.

A lady leading a dog by a leash went by. The dog strained in the direction of the man sitting on the crate. His tail wagged. The lady pulled the dog away. "Heel!" she commanded.

The dog—tail between his legs—scampered to the lady's side. Even so, the dog twisted around to look back at the beggar.

Willie grinned. The dog had done exactly what Willie had done when his mother told him not to stare.

Pressing deep into his pocket, Willie found a nickel. It was warm and slippery. He wondered how much happiness you could rent for a nickel.

Squeezing the nickel between his fingers, Willie walked slowly toward the man. When he came before him, he stopped, suddenly nervous. The man, who appeared to be looking at the ground, did not move his eyes. He smelled bad.

"Here." Willie stretched forward and dropped the coin into the man's open right hand.

"God bless you," the man said hoarsely as he folded his fingers over the coin. His eyes, like high beams on a car, flashed up at Willie, then dropped.

Willie waited for a moment, then went back up to his room. From his window he looked down on the street. He thought he saw the coin in the man's hand, but was not sure.

After supper Mrs. Markham readied herself to go to work, then kissed Willie good night. As she did every night, she said, "If you have regular problems, call Mrs. Murphy downstairs. What's her number?"

"274-8676," Willie said.

"Extra bad problems, call Grandma."

"369-6754."

"Super special problems, you can call me."

"962-6743."

"Emergency, the police."

"911."

"Lay out your morning clothing."

"I will."

"Don't let anyone in the door."

"I won't."

"No television past nine."

"I know."

"But you can read late."

"You're the one who's going to be late," Willie reminded her.

"I'm leaving," Mrs. Markham said.

After she went, Willie stood for a long while in the hallway. The empty apartment felt like a cave that lay deep below the earth. That day in school Willie's teacher had told the class about a kind of fish that lived in caves. These fish could not see. They had no eyes. The teacher had said it was living in the dark cave that made them like that.

Willie had raised his hand and asked, "If they want to get out of the cave, can they?"

"I suppose."

"Would their eyes come back?"

"Good question," she said, but did not give an answer.

Before he went to bed, Willie took another look out the window. In the pool of light cast by the street lamp, Willie saw the man.

On Tuesday morning when Willie went to school, the man was gone. But when he came home from school with his mother, he was there again.

"*Please* don't look at him," his mother whispered with some urgency.

During his snack, Willie said, "Why shouldn't I look?"

"What are you talking about?"

"That man. On the street. Begging."

"I told you. He's sick. It's better to act as if you never saw him. When people are that way they don't wish to be looked at."

"Why not?"

Mrs. Markham pondered for a while. "People are ashamed of being unhappy."

Willie looked thoughtfully at his mother. "Are you sure he's unhappy?"

"You don't have to ask if people are unhappy. They tell you all the time."

"How?"

"The way they look."

"Is that part of the sickness?"

"Oh, Willie, I don't know. It's just the way they are."

Willie contemplated the half-inch slice of cake his mother had just given him. A year ago his parents seemed to be perfectly happy. For Willie, the world seemed easy, full of light. Then his father lost his job. He tried to get another but could not. For long hours he sat in dark rooms. Sometimes he drank. His parents began to argue a lot. One day, his father was gone.

For two weeks his mother kept to the dark. And wept.

Willie looked at his mother. "You're unhappy," he said. "Are *you* ashamed?"

Mrs. Markham sighed and closed her eyes. "I wish you wouldn't ask that."

"Why?"

"It hurts me."

"But are you ashamed?" Willie persisted. He felt it was urgent that he know. So that he could do something.

She only shook her head.

Willie said, "Do you think Dad might come back?"

She hesitated before saying, "Yes, I think so."

Willie wondered if that was what she really thought.

"Do you think Dad is unhappy?" Willie asked.

"Where do you get such questions?"

"They're in my mind."

"There's much in the mind that need not be paid attention to."

"Fish who live in caves have no eyes."

"What are you talking about?"

"My teacher said it's all that darkness. The fish

forget how to see. So they lose their eyes."

"I doubt she said that."

"She did."

"Willie, you have too much imagination."

After his mother went to work, Willie gazed down onto the street. The man was there. Willie thought of going down, but he knew he was not supposed to leave the building when his mother worked at night. He decided to speak to the man the next day.

That afternoon — Wednesday — Willie stood before the man. "I don't have any money," Willie said. "Can I still talk to you?"

The man lifted his face. It was a dirty face with very tired eyes. He needed a shave.

"My mother," Willie began, "said you were unhappy. Is that true?"

"Could be," the man said.

"What are you unhappy about?"

The man's eyes narrowed as he studied Willie intently. He said, "How come you want to know?"

Willie shrugged.

"I think you should go home, kid."

"I am home." Willie gestured toward the apartment. "I live right here. Fifth floor. Where do you live?"

"Around."

"*Are* you unhappy?" Willie persisted.

The man ran a tongue over his lips. His Adam's apple bobbed. "A man has the right to remain silent," he said, and closed his eyes.

Willie remained standing on the pavement for a while before retreating back to his apartment. Once inside he looked down from the window. The man was still there. For a moment Willie was certain the man was looking at the apartment building and the floor where Willie lived.

The next day, Thursday—after dropping a nickel in the man's palm—Willie said, "I've never seen anyone look so unhappy as you do. So I figure you must know a lot about it."

The man took a deep breath. "Well, yeah, maybe."

Willie said, "And I need to find a cure for it."

"A *what?*"

"A cure for unhappiness."

The man pursed his cracked lips and blew a silent whistle. Then he said, "Why?"

"My mother is unhappy."

"Why's that?"

"My dad went away."

"How come?"

"I think because he was unhappy. Now my mother's unhappy too—all the time. So if I found a cure for unhappiness, it would be a good thing, wouldn't it?"

"I suppose. Hey, you don't have anything to eat on you, do you?"

Willie shook his head, then said, "Would you like some cake?"

"What kind?"

"I don't know. Cake."

"Depends on the cake."

On Friday Willie said to the man, "I found out what kind of cake it is."

"Yeah?"

"Pound cake. But I don't know why it's called that."

"Long as it's cake it probably don't matter."

Neither spoke. Then Willie said, "In school my teacher said there are fish who live in caves and the caves are so dark the fish don't have eyes. What do you think? Do you believe that?"

"Sure."

"You do? How come?"

"Because you said so."

"You mean, just because someone *said* it you believe it?"

"Not someone. You."

Willie was puzzled. "But, well, maybe it *isn't* true."

The man grunted. "Hey, do you believe it?"

Willie nodded.

"Well, you're not just anyone. You got eyes. You see. You ain't no fish."

"Oh." Willie was pleased.

"What's your name?" the man asked.

"Willie."

"That's a boy's name. What's your grown-up name?"

"William."

"And that means another thing."

"What?"

"I'll take some of that cake."

Willie started. "You will?" he asked, surprised.

"Just said it, didn't I?"

Willie suddenly felt excited. It was as if the man had given him a gift. Willie wasn't sure what it was except that it was important and he was glad to have it. For a moment he just gazed at the man. He saw the lines on the man's face, the way his lips curved, the small scar on the side of his chin, the shape of his eyes, which he now saw were blue.

"I'll get the cake," Willie cried and ran back to the apartment. He snatched the box from the refrigerator as well as a knife, then hurried back down to the street. "I'll cut you a piece," he said, and he opened the box.

"Hey, that don't look like a pound of cake," the man said.

Willie, alarmed, looked up.

"But like I told you, it don't matter."

Willie held his thumb against the cake to make sure the portion was the right size. With a poke of the knife he made a small mark for the proper width.

Just as he was about to cut, the man said, "Hold it!"

Willie looked up. "What?"

"What were you doing there with your thumb?"

"I was measuring the size. The right portion. A person is supposed to get only one portion."

"Where'd you learn that?"

"It says so on the box. You can see for yourself." He held out the box.

The man studied the box then handed it back to Willie. "That's just lies," he said.

"How do you know?"

"William, how can a box say how much a person needs?"

"But it does. The scientists say so. They measured, so they know. Then they put it there."

"Lies," the man repeated.

Willie began to feel that this man knew many things. "Well, then, how much should I cut?" he asked.

The man said, "You have to look at me, then at the cake, and then you're going to have to decide for yourself."

"Oh." Willie looked at the cake. The piece was about three inches wide. Willie looked up at the man. After a moment he cut the cake into two pieces, each an inch and a half wide. He gave one piece to the man and kept the other in the box.

"God bless you," the man said as he took the piece and laid it in his left hand. He began to break off pieces with his right hand and put them in his mouth one by one. Each piece was chewed thoughtfully. Willie watched him eat.

When the man was done, he licked the crumbs on his fingers.

"Now I'll give you something," the man said.

"What?" Willie said, surprised.

"The cure for unhappiness."

"You know it?" Willie asked, eyes wide.

The man nodded.

"What is it?"

"It's this: What a person needs is always more than they say."

"Who's *they*?" Willie asked.

The man pointed to the cake box. "The people on the box," he said.

In his mind Willie repeated what he had been told, then he gave the man the second piece of cake.

The man took it, saying, "Good man," and he ate it.

Willie grinned.

The next day was Saturday. Willie did not go to school. All morning he kept looking down from his window for the man, but it was raining and he did not appear. Willie wondered where he was, but could not imagine it.

Willie's mother woke about noon. Willie sat with her while she ate her breakfast. "I found the cure for unhappiness," he announced.

"Did you?" his mother said. She was reading a memo from the convenience store's owner.

"It's 'What a person needs is always more than they say.'"

His mother put her papers down. "That's nonsense. Where did you hear that?"

"That man."

"What man?"

"On the street. The one who was begging. You said he was unhappy. So I asked him."

"Willie, I told you I didn't want you to even look at that man."

"He's a nice man. . . ."

"How do you know?"

"I've talked to him."

"When? How much?"

Willie shrank down. "I did, that's all."

"Willie, I forbid you to talk to him. Do you understand me? Do you? Answer me!" She was shrill.

"Yes," Willie said, but he'd already decided he would talk to the man one more time. He needed to explain why he could not talk to him anymore.

On Sunday, however, the man was not there. Nor was he there on Monday.

"That man is gone," Willie said to his mother as they walked home from school.

"I saw. I'm not blind."

"Where do you think he went?"

"I couldn't care less. But you might as well know, I arranged for him to be gone."

Willie stopped short. "What do you mean?"

"I called the police. We don't need a nuisance like that around here. Pestering kids."

"He wasn't pestering me."

"Of course he was."

"How do you know?"

"Willie, I have eyes. I can see."

Willie glared at his mother. "No, you can't. You're a fish. You live in a cave."

"Fish?" retorted Mrs. Markham. "What do fish have to do with anything? Willie, don't talk nonsense."

"My name isn't Willie. It's William. And I know how to keep from being unhappy. I do!" He was yelling now. "What a person needs is always more than they say! *Always!*"

He turned on his heel and walked back toward the school. At the corner he glanced back. His mother was following. He kept going. She kept following.

THE GOODNESS OF MATT KAIZER

People are always saying, "Nothing's worse than when a kid goes bad." Well, let me tell you, going good isn't all that great either. Tell you what I mean.

Back in sixth grade there was a bunch of us who liked nothing better than doing bad stuff. I don't know why. We just liked doing it. And the baddest of the bad was Matt Kaizer.

Matt was a tall, thin kid with long, light blond hair that reached his shoulders. He was twelve years old — like I was. His eyes were pale blue and his skin was a

vanilla cream that never—no matter the season—
seemed to darken, except with dirt. What with the
way he looked—so pale and all—plus the fact that he
was into wearing extra large blank white T-shirts that
reached his knees, we called him "Spirit."

Now, there are two important things you need to
know about Matt Kaizer. The first was that as far as
he was concerned there was nothing good about him
at all. Nothing. The second thing was that his father
was a minister.

Our gang—I'm Marley, and then there was Chuck,
Todd, and Nick—loved the fact that Matt was so
bad and his father a minister. You know, we were
always daring him to do bad things. "Hey, minister's
kid!" we'd taunt. "Dare you to . . ." and we'd
challenge him to do something, you know, really
gross. Thing is, we could always count on Matt—
who wanted to show he wasn't good—to take a
dare.

For instance: Say there was some dead animal out

on the road. We'd all run to Matt and say, "Dare you to pick it up."

Matt would look at it — up close and personal — or more than likely poke it with a stick, then pick it up and fling it at one of us.

Disgusting stories? Someone would tell one and then say, "Dare you to tell it to Mary Beth Bataky"— the class slug—and Matt would tell it to her—better than anyone else, too.

TV and movies? The more blood and gore there was, the more Matt ate it up—if you know what I mean. MTV, cop shows, all that bad stuff, nothing was too gross for him.

And it didn't take just dares to get Matt going. No, Matt would do stuff on his own. If anyone blew a toot—even in class—he would bellow, "Who cut the cheese?" He could belch whenever he wanted to, and did, a lot. Spitballs, booger flicking, wedgie yanking, it was all wicked fun for Matt. No way was he going to be good! Not in front of us.

Now, his father, the minister, "Rev. Kaizer" we
called him, wasn't bad. In fact just the opposite. The
guy was easygoing, always dressed decently, and as
far as I knew, never raised his voice or acted any way
than what he was, a nice man, a good man. Sure, he
talked a little funny, like he was reading from a book,
but that was all.

Did Matt and his father get along? In a way. For
example, once I was with Matt after he did something
bad—I think he blew his nose on someone's lunch.
Rev. Kaizer had learned about it. Instead of getting
mad he just gazed at Matt, shook his head, and said,
"Matt, I do believe there's goodness in everyone. That
goes for you too. Someday you'll find your own goodness. And when you do you'll be free."

"I'm not good," Matt insisted.

"Well, I think you are," his father said, patiently.

Matt grinned. "Long as my friends dare me to do
bad things, I'll do 'em."

"Never refuse a dare?" his father asked, sadly.

"Never," Matt said with pride.

Rev. Kaizer sighed, pressed his hands together, and looked toward heaven.

So there we were, a bunch of us who knew we were bad and that it was doing bad things that held us together. And the baddest of the bad, like I said, was Matt — the Spirit — Kaizer. But then . . . oh, man, I'll tell you what happened.

One day after school we were hanging out in the playground. The five of us were just sitting around telling disgusting stories, when suddenly Chuck said, "Hey, hear about Mary Beth Bataky?"

"What about her?" Matt asked.

"Her old man's dying."

Right away Matt was interested. "Really?"

"It's true, man," Chuck insisted. "He's just about had it."

"How come?" I asked.

"Don't know," said Chuck. "He's sick. So sick they sent him home from the hospital. That's why

Mary Beth is out. She's waiting for him to die."

"Cool," said Matt.

Now, Mary Beth was one small straw of a sad slug. She had this bitsy face with pale eyes and two gray lines for lips all framed in a pair of frizzy braids. Her arms were thin and always crossed over her chest, which was usually bundled in a brown sweater. The only bits of color on her were her fingernails, which, though chewed, were spotted with bright red nail polish — chipped.

So when we heard what was going on with Mary Beth and her father, we guys eyed one another, almost knowing what was going to happen next. But, I admit, it was me who said, "Hey, Spirit, I dare you to go and see him."

Matt pushed the blond hair out of his face and looked at us with those pale blue, cool-as-ice eyes of his.

"Or maybe," Todd said, "you're too chicken, being as you're a minister's kid and all."

That did it. Course it did. No way Matt could resist a dare. He got up, casual like. "I'll do it," he said. "Who's coming with me?"

To my disgust the other guys backed off. But I accepted. Well, actually, I really didn't think he'd do it.

But then, soon as we started off, I began to feel a little nervous. "Matt," I warned. "I think Mary Beth is very religious."

"Don't worry. I know about all that stuff."

"Yeah, but what would your father say?"

"I don't care," he bragged. "Anyway, I'm not going to *do* anything except look. It'll be neat. Like a horror movie. Maybe I can even touch the guy. A dying body is supposed to be colder than ice."

That was Matt. Always taking up the dare and going you one worse.

The more he talked the sorrier I was we had dared him to go. Made me really uncomfortable. Which I think he noticed, because he said, "What's the matter, Marley? You scared or something?"

"Just seems . . ."

"I know," he taunted, "you're too good!" He belched loudly to make his point that he wasn't. "See you later, dude." He started off.

I ran after him. "Do you know where she lives?"

"Follow me."

"They might not let you see him," I warned.

He pulled out some coins. "I'm going to buy some flowers and bring them to him. That's what my mother did when my aunt was sick." He stuffed his mouth full of bubble gum and began blowing and popping.

Mary Beth's house was a wooden three-decker with a front porch. Next to the front door were three bell buttons with plastic name labels. The Batakys lived on the first floor.

By the time Matt and I got there he had two wilted carnations in his hand. One was dyed blue, the other green. The flower store guy had sold them for ten cents each.

"You know," I said in a whisper, as we stood before the door, "her father might already be dead."

"Cool," Matt replied, blowing another bubble, while cleaning out an ear with a pinky and inspecting the earwax carefully before smearing it on his shirt. "Did you know your fingernails still grow when you're dead? Same for your hair. I mean, how many really dead people can you get to see?" he said and rang the Batakys' bell.

From far off inside there was a buzzing sound.

I was trying to get the nerve to leave when the door opened a crack. Mary Beth — pale eyes rimmed with red — peeked out. There were tears on her cheeks and her lips were crusty. Her small hands — with their spots of red fingernail polish — were trembling.

"Oh, hi," she said, her voice small and tense.

I felt tight with embarrassment.

Matt spoke out loudly. "Hi, Mary Beth. We heard your old man was dying."

"Yes, he is," Mary Beth murmured. With one hand

on the doorknob it was pretty clear she wanted to retreat as fast as possible. "He's delirious."

"Delirious?" Matt said. "What's that?"

"Sort of . . . crazy."

"Oh . . . wow, sweet!" he said, giving me a nudge of appreciation. Then he held up the blue and green carnations, popped his gum, and said, "I wanted to bring him these."

Mary Beth stared at the flowers, but didn't move to take them. All she said was, "My mother's at St. Mary's, praying."

Now I really wanted to get out of there. But Matt said, "How about if I gave these to your father?" He held up the flowers again. "Personally."

"My mother said he may die any moment," Mary Beth informed us.

"I know," Matt said. "So I'd really like to see him before he does."

Mary Beth gazed at him. "He's so sick," she said, "he's not up to visiting."

"Yeah," Matt pressed, "but, you see, the whole class elected me to come and bring these flowers."

His lie worked. "Oh," Mary Beth murmured, and she pulled the door open. "Well, I suppose . . ."

We stepped into a small entrance way. A low-watt bulb dangled over our heads from a wire. Shoes, boots, and broken umbrellas lay in a plastic milk crate.

Mary Beth shut the outside door then pushed open an inner one that led to her apartment. It was gloomy and stank of medicine.

Matt bopped me on the arm. "Who cut the cheese!" he said with a grin. I looked around at him. He popped another bubble.

"Down this way," Mary Beth whispered.

We walked down a long hallway. Two pictures were on the walls. They were painted on black velvet. One was a scene of a mountain with snow on it and the sun shining on a stag with antlers. The second picture was of a little girl praying by her bed. Fuzzy gold light streamed in on her from a window.

At the end of the hall was a closed door. Mary Beth halted. "He's in here," she whispered. "He's really sick," she warned again. "And he doesn't notice anyone. You really sure you want to see him?"

"You bet," Matt said with enthusiasm.

"I mean, he won't say hello or anything," Mary Beth said in her low voice. "He just lies there with his eyes open. I don't even know if he sees anything."

"Does he have running sores?" Matt asked.

I almost gagged.

"Running *what*?" Mary Beth asked.

"You know, wounds."

"It's his liver," Mary Beth explained sadly, while turning the door handle and opening the door. "The doctor said it was all his bad life and drinking."

Dark as the hall had been, her father's room was darker. The air was heavy and really stank. A large bed took up most of the space. On one side of the bed was a small chest of drawers. On top of the chest was a lit candle and a glass of water into which a pair of false teeth had been dropped. On the other side of the bed was a wooden chair. Another burning candle was on that.

On the bed—beneath a brown blanket—lay Mr. Bataky. He was stretched out on his back perfectly straight, like a log. His head and narrow chest were propped up on a pile of four pillows with pictures of flowers on them. At the base of the bed his toes poked up from under the blanket. He was clothed in pajamas dotted with different colored hearts. His hands—looking like a bunch of knuckles—were linked over his chest. His poorly shaven face—yellow in color—was thin. With his cheeks sunken, his nose seemed enormous. His thin hair was uncombed. His breathing was drawn out, almost whistling, and collapsed into throat gargles—as if he were choking.

Worst of all, his eyes were open but he was just staring up, like he was waiting for something to happen in heaven.

Mary Beth stepped to one side of the bed. Matt

stood at the foot, with me peering over his shoulder. We stared at the dying man. He really looked bad. Awful.

"I don't think he'll live long," Mary Beth murmured, her sad voice breaking, her tears dripping.

Matt lifted the blue and green carnations. "Mr. Bataky," he shouted, "I brought you some flowers to cheer you up."

"His hearing isn't good," Mary Beth said apologetically.

Matt looked about for a place to put the flowers, saw the glass with the teeth near Mr. Bataky's head, and moved to put them into the water. In the flickering candlelight, Matt's pale skin, his long blond hair, seemed to glow.

Now, just as Matt came up to the head of the bed, Mr. Bataky's eyes shifted. They seemed to fasten on Matt. The old man gave a start, made a convulsive twitch as his eyes positively bulged. Matt, caught in the look, froze.

"It's . . . it's . . . an *angel.* . . ," Mr. Bataky said in a low, rasping voice. "An angel . . . from heaven has come to save me."

Matt lifted his hand — the one that held the carnations — and tried to place them in the glass of water. Before he could, Mr. Bataky made an unexpected jerk with one of his knobby hands and took hold of Matt's arm. Matt was so surprised he dropped the flowers.

"Father!" Mary Beth cried.

"Thank . . . you . . . for coming, Angel," Mr. Bataky rasped.

"No . . . really," Matt stammered, "I'm not — "

"Yes, you're an angel," Mr. Bataky whispered. His eyes — full of tears — were hot with joy.

Matt turned red. "No, I'm not . . ."

"Please," Mr. Bataky cried out with amazing energy, "I don't want to die bad." Tears gushed down his hollow cheeks. "You got to help me. Talk to me. Bless me."

Matt, speechless for once, gawked at the man.

With considerable effort he managed to pry Mr. Bataky's fingers from his arm. Soon as he did he bolted from the room.

"Don't abandon me!" Mr. Bataky begged, somehow managing to lift himself up and extend his arms toward the doorway. "Don't!"

Frightened, I hurried out after Matt.

My buddy was waiting outside, breathing hard. His normally pale face was paler than ever. As we walked away he didn't say anything.

Now, according to Matt — he told us all this later — what happened was that night Rev. Kaizer called him into his study.

"Matt, please sit down."

Matt, thinking he was going to get a lecture about visiting Mary Beth's house, sat.

His father said, "Matt, I think it's quite wonderful what you've done, going to the home of your classmate's dying father to comfort him."

"What do you mean?" Matt asked.

Rev. Kaizer smiled sweetly. "A woman by the name of Mrs. Bataky called me. She said her husband was very ill. Dying. She said you—I gather you go to school with her daughter—came to visit him today. Apparently her husband thought you were an . . . angel. It's the first real sign of life her poor husband has shown in three days. And now, Matt, he's quite desperate to see the angel—you—again."

"It's not true," Matt rapped out.

"Now, Matt," his father said, "I found the woman's story difficult to believe, too. 'Madam,' I said to her, 'are you quite certain you're talking about *my* son? And are you truly saying your husband really thought he was . . . an angel?'

"And she said, 'Rev. Kaizer—you being a minister I can say it—my husband led a bad, sinful life. But there's something about your son that's making him want to talk about it. Sort of like a confession. Know what I'm saying? I mean, it would do him a lot of good. What I'm asking is, could you get your son to come again? I'm really scared my husband will get worse if he doesn't.'"

"Matt," said Rev. Kaizer, "I'm proud of you. I think it would be a fine thing if you visited him again."

"I'm not an angel," Matt replied in a sulky voice.

"I never said *you* were an angel," his father said. "But as I've told you many times, there is goodness inside you as there is in everyone. And now you are in the fortunate position of being able to help this sinful man."

"I don't want to."

"Son, here is a sick man who needs to unburden himself of the unhappy things he's done. I know your reputation. Are you fearful of hearing what Mr. Bataky has to say for himself?"

"I don't want to."

Rev. Kaizer sat back in his chair, folded his hands over his stomach, smiled gently, and said, "I dare you to go back and listen to Mr. Bataky. I dare you to do goodness."

Alarmed, Matt looked up. "But . . ."

"Or are you, being a minister's son, afraid to?"

Matt shifted uncomfortably in his seat and tried to avoid his father's steady gaze.

Rev. Kaizer offered up a faint smile. "Matt, I thought you never refused a dare."

Matt squirmed. Then he said, "I'll go."

Anyway, that's the way Matt explained it all. And as he said to me, sadly, "What choice did I have? He dared me."

We all saw then that Matt was in a bad place.

So the next day when Matt went to visit Mr. Bataky, the bunch of us — me, Chuck, Todd, and Nick — tagged along. We all wanted to see what Matt would do. We figured it *had* to be gross.

Mary Beth opened the door. I think she was surprised to see all of us. But she looked at Matt with hope. "Thank you for coming," she said in her tissue paper voice. "He's waiting for you."

Matt gave us an imploring look. There was

nothing we could do. He disappeared inside. We waited outside.

Half an hour later, when he emerged, there was a ton of worry in his eyes. We waited him out, hoping he'd say something ghastly. Didn't say a word.

Two blocks from Mary Beth's house I couldn't hold back. "Okay, Matt," I said. "What's happening?"

Matt stopped walking. "He really thinks I'm a good angel."

"How come?" Nick asked.

"I don't know." There was puzzlement in Matt's voice. "He thinks I'm there to give him a second chance at living."

"I don't get it," Todd said.

Matt said, "He thinks, you know, if he tells me all his bad stuff, he'll get better."

We walked on in silence. Then I said—easy like, "He tell you anything, you know . . . really bad?"

Matt nodded.

"Oooo, that's so cool," Nick crowed, figuring Matt

would—as he always did—pass it on. "Like what?"

Instead of answering, Matt remained silent. Finally, he said, "Not good."

"Come on!" we cried. "Tell us!"

"He dared me to forgive him. To give him a second chance."

"Forgive him for what?" I asked.

"All the stuff he's done."

"Like what?"

"He said he was talking to me . . . in confidence."

"What's that mean?"

"Angels can't tell secrets."

"You going to believe that?" Todd asked after a bit of silence.

Matt stopped walking again. "But . . . what," he stammered. "What . . . if it's true?"

"What if *what's* true?" I asked.

"What if I'm really good inside?"

"No way," we all assured him.

"But he thinks so," Matt said with real trouble in

his voice. "And my father is always saying that too."

"Do *you* think so?" Chuck asked.

Matt got a flushed look in his eyes. Then he said, "If it is true, it'll be the grossest thing ever."

"Hey, maybe it's just a phase," I suggested, hopefully. "You know, something you'll grow out of."

Matt gave a shake to his head that suggested he was really seriously confused.

Anyway, every afternoon that week, Matt went to see Mr. Bataky. Each time we went with him. For support. We felt we owed him that, though really, we were hoping we'd get to hear some of the bad stuff. But I think we were getting more and more upset, too. See, Matt was changing. Each time he came out of the sick man's room, he looked more and more haggard. And silent.

"What did he say this time?" someone would finally ask.

"Really bad," he'd say.

"Worse than before?"

"Much worse."

We'd go on for a bit, not saying anything. Then the pleading would erupt. "Come on! Tell us! What'd he say?"

"Can't."

"Why?"

"I told you: He thinks I'm an angel," Matt said and visibly shuddered. "Angels can't tell secrets."

As the week progressed, Matt began to look different from before. He wasn't so grubby. His clothes weren't torn. Things went so fast that by Friday morning, when he came to school, he was actually wearing a tie! Even his hair was cut short and combed. It was awful.

"What's the matter with Matt?" we kept asking one another.

"I think he's beginning to think he really is an angel," was the only explanation I could give.

Finally, on Friday afternoon, when Matt came out of Mary Beth's house, he sat on the front steps, utterly beat. By that time he was dressed all in white: white shirt, pale tie, white pants, and even white sneakers. Not one smudge on him. I'm telling you, it was eerie. Nothing missing but wings.

"What's up?" I asked.

"The doctor told Mr. Bataky he's better."

"You cured him!" cried Nick. "Cool! That mean you don't have to visit him again?"

"Right." But Matt just sat there looking as sad as Mary Beth ever did.

"What's the matter?" I asked.

"I've been sitting and listening to that guy talk and talk about all the things he's done. I mean, I used to think I was bad. But, you know what?"

"What?"

"I'm not bad. No way. Not compared to him. I even tried to tell him of some of the things I've done."

"What did he say?"

"He laughed. Said I was only a young angel. Which was the reason I didn't have wings."

Matt stared down at the ground for a long time. We waited patiently. Finally he looked up. There were tears trickling down his pale face.

"I have to face it," he said, turning to look at us, his pals, with real grief in his eyes. "The more I heard that stuff Mr. Bataky did, the more I knew that deep down, inside, I'm just a good kid. I mean, what am I going to do? Don't you see, I'm just like my father said. I'm *good.*"

You can't believe how miserable he looked. All we could do was sit there and pity him. I mean, just to look at him we knew there weren't going to be any more wicked grins, belches, leers, sly winks, wedgies, or flying boogers.

Life went on, but with Matt going angel on us, our gang couldn't hold together. We were finished. Busted.

So I'm here to tell you, when a guy turns good, hey, it's rough.

TALK TO ME

At exactly four o'clock one Tuesday afternoon, Maria O'Sullivan's own personal phone rang. Absorbed in her sixth-grade history, Maria let it ring a few times, then bounded across her room to snatch up the phone before the answering machine kicked in.

"Hello?" she said.

There was no reply. Not a whisper. Not a sound.

"Hello?" Maria said again.

For a second she actually thought someone was at the other end listening, but the next moment there

was a click and the other party—whoever it was—
hung up.

Only a little annoyed, Maria promptly put her
phone down and returned to her desk. Briefly, she
glanced at her clock by the phone. One minute after
four. Her mom would be back from work in an hour.
Her dad would be home shortly after. She was glad.
Being in an empty house—as Maria was most days
after school—made her feel lonely. Happily, with
homework to absorb her, she settled back down.

On Thursday after school, Maria had invited her new
classmate, Sophie, over. Sophie had not visited before.
The two girls listened to the radio, chatted, gossiped,
looked through Sophie's bundle of teen magazines.
There was a lot of giggling.

At precisely four o'clock the phone rang.

Maria jumped for it. "Hello?" she said.

There was no answer.

"Hello?"

There was still no reply.

Maria hung up. "I hate it," she said, "when people get a wrong number and just say nothing. So rude."

"I know. . . ," Sophie said, gazing at the high cheekbones of a model in a magazine.

"Happens here a lot," Maria mused.

"It would be so cool to look like that," Sophie said and she pouted, imitating a blonde female model.

Maria glanced at Sophie. Then she said, "My brother was blond."

Sophie bent over the magazine. "My mother said I could come here but . . . only if I didn't talk about your brother."

Maria flushed. "How does she know about Brian?"

"I don't know," Sophie said vaguely. "I guess . . . people told her . . . something."

Maria said, "But *why* did your mother say you mustn't talk about him?"

"Your brother was . . . weird, wasn't he?" Then,

giggling, Sophie added, "I guess she thinks he might be a bad influence."

Maria managed to say, "But he's not here."

Sophie shrugged. "This guy is so cute." She was scrutinizing the picture of a young movie star.

Maria knew she would not invite Sophie over again.

That evening, close to ten, Maria's mother was saying good night to her daughter when Maria asked, "Mom, why do people call wrong numbers?"

Sarah O'Sullivan laughed. "Sweetheart, they're called wrong numbers because people have made a mistake. They don't mean to do it."

"I suppose."

"How did you get along with that Sophie? She seemed very nice."

Maria's face clouded. "I don't like her."

"Maria, it's important to have friends. You have so few."

"She said her mother told her she wasn't allowed to talk to me about Brian. She's not the only one."

Mrs. O'Sullivan sighed. "Sometimes I think it would be better if we moved."

"Then Brian wouldn't be able to find us."

Mrs. O'Sullivan considered her daughter, then bent over and gave her a good night kiss. Maria wasn't fooled. Her talk of Brian had upset her mother.

"Why does no one want to talk about Brian?" Maria asked.

Her mother said nothing.

"You won't," Maria said.

"Maria, there's little to say. He's gone. Should I send Dad in to say good night?"

"No. He won't talk, either," Maria said angrily. "I'd rather be alone." She closed her eyes.

"Good night, sweet. I love you." There was sadness in Mrs. O'Sullivan's voice.

"Night. . . ," Maria murmured.

As Mrs. O'Sullivan left the room, she turned out the lights.

A few months ago Maria had stuck luminescent stars on the ceiling. For a short time after her lights were turned out at night, they glowed with a soft green shimmer. Now, as she gazed up at them, she regretted having said that she wanted to be alone. She hated being alone.

It was when she was alone that she thought most about Brian. It was almost a year now since her older brother had left home. Maria never fully understood why he had gone. True, he had been having lots of fights with their parents, but mostly with their dad. About when to come home. Drinking. Not telling the truth. Even stealing. Then suddenly — without warning — he had gone, disappeared. He was sixteen.

When Maria thought about her brother it made her heart ache. She kept wishing she knew where he was. At first Maria had continued to ask her parents if they had heard anything. They always said no. She was not sure she believed them.

Lately she realized she had begun to forget what Brian looked like. It gave her a panicky feeling. She'd dug up old photos of Brian and studied them, looking for clues.

When she did think of him she always thought about him in a particular way: jeans, yellow sneakers, and a bright red T-shirt that revealed his new fire-breathing dragon arm tattoo. The tattoo had outraged her parents. But that was the way he had looked for her last birthday party.

More than anything, Maria wished she could talk to someone about Brian. If she talked to her dad, he cut her off by changing the subject. If she spoke to her mom, Mrs. O'Sullivan became upset and walked away. As for her classmates, Maria had tried, as she had tried with Sophie. People just did not want to talk about Brian. It was as if her brother, by running away from home, had become dangerous.

It gave Maria a great deal of pain. The pain only

seemed to build. She would have given anything to share it with someone. Anyone.

"Brian," Maria whispered to the fading stars as she drifted off to sleep, "talk to me."

It was not until the following Monday that a call came again. Precisely at four. Maria was sprawled on her bed, reading. The ringing startled her. It was when she began to reach for the phone that she noticed the clock and the time. Only then did she grasp that the phone had rung twice before at exactly the same time — four o'clock.

Suddenly tense, she said, "Hello?"

There was no answer.

"Who are you?" Maria demanded.

No sound of breathing, or anything.

She said, "I know you're there."

The caller hung up.

Maria cradled the phone in her hands for a while, trying to guess who it might be. After all, it was her own private line with its own listing. Whoever was calling could be calling only her. She wondered who in school would play a prank like that. One of the boys, probably. Like Jeff. She liked Jeff. He was always into mischief. Then suddenly a new thought came to Maria: Maybe it's Brian. Her skin prickled at the notion.

"Brian . . . ?" she whispered, almost as if trying a new word.

No response.

Slowly—Maria's hand shook a little—she hung up the phone. "That's so dumb," she scolded herself. "You just want it to be him."

Maria made herself read her book. Later on, she didn't remember what she had read. She did remember the call.

During the next few afternoons when it drew close to four o'clock, Maria hung around the phone. It did not ring. When Maria realized she was disappointed she scolded herself. "You are *such* a jerk. You think it might be Brian," she said to herself. "It's not. He's gone."

When after a few days passed and no further calls came, she made herself stay out of the house at four: She went to the library or even walked the dog.

On Friday she was home, alone. At precisely four o'clock the phone rang.

Maria gazed at the phone as it continued to ring. The answering machine would turn on after four rings. "I shouldn't answer," she told herself. Maria counted the rings. ". . . two . . . three . . . four . . ." She snatched up the phone.

"Hello?"

There was no answer.

"You keep calling at four o'clock," Maria snapped. "Is this Jeff?"

There was no answer.

"I mean . . . *who are you*!" Maria shouted, with a sudden surge of anger.

"I'm going to tell the police!" she cried and slammed the phone down.

Maria sat on the edge of her bed, trembling. She recalled her dad's stern lecture about strange, obscene, and even automatic telemarketing calls. He had told her not to talk to strangers but to hang up and call him.

Instead, Maria rang her mother at the shipping company office where she worked.

"What's up, honey?"

"Nothing. I just wanted to say hello."

"Glad you did. You sound upset. Everything okay?"

"Yeah."

"See you soon. Dad will be there soon."

"Bye."

It was not until two weeks later that another call came. Maria had almost forgotten about them. Now when the phone rang, her eyes went right to the clock. Four o'clock, exactly. Heart pounding, she reminded herself yet again that it was a mistake to pick up the phone. But she did so on the fourth ring.

"Hello?" she said, cautiously.

There was no answer.

"I know this isn't a wrong number," Maria said with irritation. "I mean, you keep calling. Would you just tell me who you are?"

There was no answer.

"You are so dumb!" she shouted into the phone.

Whoever was on the other end did not hang up.

"Are you a boy or a girl? A man or a woman? Talk to me!"

No response.

"What do you want?" Maria asked plaintively.

There was click at the other end.

Maria flung the phone down, then threw herself on her bed, buried her face in a pillow, and began to cry.

"Maria, honey, are you all right?"

She had fallen asleep. Her father was bending over her.

Fred O'Sullivan was tall and strong with thick gray curly hair that sometimes made Maria think of a kitchen scrub pad. His eyes were dark, his mouth tight. Sometimes there could be a sternness — a way he clenched his jaw when he had made up his mind — that told Maria it was useless to argue with him. At the moment, however, he looked worried.

Maria blinked and sat up. "Just tired," she said.

"Hard day at school?"

"Sort of . . ." Maria looked up at her father. She wished she would not blame him for Brian's going. She did though. All that arguing, fighting, lecturing. Maria believed it was that which drove Brian away.

"Want to talk about it?" her dad asked softly. He was sitting on the edge of the bed, one hand resting gently on Maria's hand.

"I want to talk about Brian," she said.

Mr. O'Sullivan's jaw clenched. It was gone in a moment. He smiled. Maria thought it was forced. "Brian is gone," he said. "There's no point in talking about him. How about you and I going out for ice cream after dinner?" he asked.

Maria hesitated. "Can Mom come too?"

"Well . . . sure," he said, sounding disappointed. "You ask her." He bent forward as if he meant to kiss Maria. Maria, not really meaning to, shifted slightly. Her father froze.

After dinner they did go for ice cream, all three of them. Maria tried to be happy, chatting brightly about school. After a while she decided it was all empty talk. She fell into silence. No one spoke.

Each afternoon at four o'clock Maria waited by the phone, hoping it would ring. When it didn't she felt disappointment, then frustration. Disappointment because she wanted desperately to be called. Frustration because she knew she wanted it to be Brian.

But — as she kept telling herself — it couldn't be him, not really.

Still, she was sure of one thing. Whoever was calling really wanted to reach her. After all, he — if it was a he — kept trying. But who was it? Why should he be doing this? Why should he care so much about reaching her?

There were times Maria felt she really must tell her parents about the calls. They were very protective, which pleased her, mostly. But she knew they would not want her to be talking, secretly, to Brian. Or to any other secret friend.

The moment Maria thought the words "secret friend," her heart beat very fast. Could the caller truly be a secret friend? Oh, how she wished the person would call now! But the phone was still.

Two days later a call came. At exactly four o'clock.

"Hello?" Maria said, hopefully.

No reply.

"You're still not going to tell me who you are, are you?" Maria said.

No answer.

"I would like to have a secret friend," Maria announced. "You know, someone to talk to."

No response.

Maria took a deep breath. "My name is Maria O'Sullivan. I'm twelve years old. I'm five foot four inches and weigh one hundred and three pounds. I've got light brown hair. Not really blonde, or anything like that. I play soccer. I like to read. And I'm good in science, but I don't like history very much. My grades are good, and I'm a nice person. I think."

Maria waited for a response. There was none.

She gripped the phone tighter and went on. "I live with my parents. My mother's name is Sarah. My father's name is Frederick. And I have — " Abruptly, Maria hung up the phone.

Maria was not sure she knew why she had hung

up. Or why she felt like crying. But the next moment she knew: It was an enormous relief to be talking to someone. Even if — she reminded herself with a giggle — she had no idea who it was.

Maria lay back on her bed and stared up at the ceiling at the stars that were not glowing. She remembered when her brother had taught her to wish by the first star she saw at night.

Star bright, star light,
First star I see tonight.
I wish I may, I wish I might,
I wish my wish would come true tonight.

"Can you wish," Maria wondered to herself, "by a phony star?"

"I told you who I was," Maria said the next time the four o'clock call came. "But I haven't told you the most important thing about me. Do you want to know?"

There was no answer.

"I'm going to tell you. Now." Maria closed her eyes. "You can hang up if you don't want to hear any of this. Like, I'd really understand. Anyway, it's this. See, my brother — his name is Brian — ran away a year ago. I'm really not sure why. I guess he and my parents just couldn't get along. There were all these arguments. Fights, really. My brother has this foul mouth. He used it too. So much tension. It was awful. My father said they didn't love each other anymore. I don't think Brian ever said that. But I'm not sure. When my brother went, he left me — and only me — a note. I came home from school and checked the mail — I always do, though I never get letters — and then I went to the kitchen. For a snack."

Maria stopped talking for a moment. It had become hard to speak.

Recovering, she said, "On the kitchen table I found a note. I still have it. I keep it in a special place. Anyway, what he wrote on that note—I know it by heart—was,

Maria . . .

I am out of here. I have to find myself.
Sorry Im hurting you by going. Love you.
Totally. But . . . I can't love you very well in
this house. Bummer. Don't ya forget me!
Your lovin' bro,

Brian

"That's all he wrote. When my parents came home I showed the note to them. Mom cried. Dad went for a long walk. Does that make any sense to you?"

There was no answer.

"I mean, Brian could have just moved out. You know, like to another part of the city. I know other families where stuff like that happened. But since he left . . . well, I haven't heard from him. At all. Not on my birthday. Or on Christmas. Not once. I'm not even sure my parents know where he is. Or if they do they won't tell me.

"And . . . I miss him so much. I think about him a lot. And worry. You know what I mean?"

There was no answer.

Maria hung up the phone slowly. Though she felt sad, it was good to talk to someone. If it was someone. She stared at the phone. She hoped it *was* someone.

"The thing about Brian," Maria was explaining to the caller three days later, "is that he was very nice to me. I mean, he liked doing things his way and all, and he never did well in school. My parents were always bugging him about working harder at it. He said he was stupid and to get off his back. He was his own person, he said, whatever that means. He said he couldn't ever learn. He used to tell me all the stuff he did, and some of it was, well, like, bad. And my parents said he was a rotten influence on me. But he wasn't. He was sweet to me. My big brother. So I'm so mad at my parents. I think they pushed him out. Mostly my dad. But I can't talk to them like I'm talking to you. It's as if they want to forget all about him. That's what's so great about you, you just listen. You just, you know, accept what I say. Like, you must be very special. I mean, you must be someone, aren't you?"

There was no answer.

Maria hung up and stared up at her stars. Maybe I'm crazy, she thought. But I know there is a person there. I know there is.

"I know I think too much about my brother," Maria explained into the phone a few days later. "But it's mostly, like, worry. I mean, maybe he's sick or in jail, and that's why he never calls or anything. What if he were dead? I mean, what's he *doing*? Does he think about me at all? Does he worry about me the way I do about him?

"Before he left I heard my father say to my mother—they didn't know I was listening—that he thought Brian was ill or something. I mean, what kind of ill? Mental or, you know, sick in bed?

"It's so scary to think about all that. I think maybe, if I just knew he was all right or really, truly gone—you know, really never coming back, ever—I could accept that. Then I wouldn't worry. I'd just accept it. That's why I'm so glad I can talk to you about him. I've tried to talk to people. But you're the first one who listens. Really listens. But talking makes me feel so much better. I think if I met you—I mean, in person—I would like you too. And I don't even know you exist!

"But, can I ask you something? Maybe, just once, you could talk. You could say yes or no, and I'd never, ever ask you again, or ask you to answer anything. Just this once. I even made a wish . . . please. I mean, I really want to know, because sometimes I think . . . want . . . wish . . . well . . . Are you Brian?"

There was no answer.

"I've been wondering what you're like," Maria said when the four o'clock call came a few days later. "I mean, look like. I'm sure of one thing. I mean, I think I am. You're a teenager. I mean, no kid—or grownup—would listen to a kid like me babble on. Right? It's so cool. I know, you won't answer. But I do think about you. I decided you are medium height. Good looking. And you have a nice smile. But shy. So you keep looking away. Something like that. And I do wonder why you have the time to listen to me. I think—tell me if I'm right—you want to be a photographer. No! You paint pictures. I figure, you don't know what I look like, but you have this imagination, so, like, you can see me.

"I do wish I could see you. Actually," Maria said, her heart suddenly pounding, "I've made up my mind that . . . that you are . . . my brother. Brian . . . *please* . . . is this you?"

There was no answer.

"Guess what?" Maria said as soon as she picked up the phone at four o'clock. "Yesterday my parents took me out for dinner — we don't usually do that school nights — and they said they were going to have a baby and asked how did I feel about it. Not as if it were up to me, but, you know, how did I feel?

"I didn't know how I felt. 'You're too old,' I said. It just popped out. They laughed. 'I guess not,' Mom said. And they did seem happy. And it is cool because I could *see* they were happy. I suppose it would be fun to have a baby in the house. They said I would be the most important person in the whole world to it, because I would be its big sister. That's so weird. Would you believe . . . big sister? I was trying to imagine it, but couldn't. Then they said they already knew it was going to be a boy. That's even weirder. But I'll tell you one thing. I'd never run away from it.

"Then later, at night, when I got into bed — and

I was looking up at my stars, I felt sort of lonely. I mean, maybe my parents wouldn't spend as much time with me. They couldn't, right? The baby and all. And since . . . it's going to be a boy, will they forget all about Brian? I suppose that's what will happen. Maybe the baby is to replace you. That made me feel so bad, 'cause I don't think that's fair. Do you have any advice for me?"

There was no answer.

Maria stared at the phone. Did she, she wondered, really believe someone was listening? "Please, please, please," she whispered, "be someone."

"I really think I should see you. I mean, if you're real. I really, really, *really* think I should. I mean, after a while my mother will be home a lot. With the baby. And then if you call the way you do, she's going to ask me who you are, and what am I supposed to say if she asks? Tell her? Then my father will find out. They tell each other everything. And he might do something. He can be strict. But if I could say who you are, and you know, I said you are this real friend. . . . Would you please, please let me see you?

"You are so important to me. I can talk to you. You're like a diary. Only, instead of writing my thoughts down, I tell them. But I don't know anything about who you are. I mean, well . . . I have decided you are Brian. But what if you're not? Will you let us meet? Once? Just for a short time?"

There was no answer.

"If you say nothing— 'cause I know you don't like to say anything— if you say nothing— that will mean yes. Okay?"

There was no reply.

"That means yes," Maria said excitedly. "It does. I think."

"I have a half day off from school next Thursday. The teachers are doing something. I didn't tell my parents. So you and I could meet. At twelve-thirty. Would you be willing to? Just once? You said you would.

"We could meet at McDonald's. There's one on Montana Boulevard, near Emerson Street. It's right on the way home from my school. Lots of kids stop there. It's big, too. Has an upstairs. I could be at a certain table. Or you could. Would you, please, pretty, pretty please with a cherry on top? I'd really love to talk to you. I mean, in person. Like, I really like you. And if I could just see you, once. Just once. And we'd just talk. Really talk. Be so cool. Just a little. I mean, I've told you things that I've never told anyone.

"Next Thursday, right? Say yes again? Please. Say yes by not saying anything."

There was no reply.

"That means yes," Maria whispered.

"Okay, tomorrow, then. I checked it out. There's this table at that McDonald's I told you about with built-in benches, you know, like they have — and it's way off in a corner on the second level. No one ever sits there. Next to the window, where, if you look out of it, you see down into the parking lot.

"But how will I know it's you? I mean, if some other person happens to be there. It would be so embarrassing.

"I know! You could be wearing something I would recognize. Actually, I've been thinking about that. A lot. And if you would wear . . . well, a red T-shirt. With your dragon tattoo showing. And jeans . . . and yellow sneakers. Sort of too bright, I know, but then I'd really know who you were. Would you, please?"

That night Maria could hardly sleep. Instead she stared at the stars.

Star bright, star light,
First star I see tonight.
I wish I may, I wish I might,
I wish my wish would come true tonight.

"I wish it's going to be you, Brian. I really, really wish it!"

As Maria walked along Montana Boulevard her heart was beating very fast. She kept brushing tears away from her eyes. And giggling. She had never thought the McDonald's was so far.

She ran the last part, bursting into the main floor and looking around for a person in a red T-shirt. There were people, but not the one she was looking for.

Finding it hard to breathe, she charged up the steps to the second floor. Her whole body trembling, she raced toward the corner table, only to stop short and stare. No one was there.

Maria sat at the table for two hours. No one came. At first she cried. Then she dried her tears and tried to think what had happened, thinking hard about her conversations with the caller. She made herself acknowledge that the caller had never said so much as one word. In the end she could admit to herself that she didn't know who had called.

Maria walked home slowly. Once inside her house she gathered the mail from inside the door. There was a letter addressed to her.

Maria O'Sullivan, Telephone Patron
She opened it up and read it.

Dear Telephone Patron,

It has been brought to our attention that the Teledine Automated Marketing Company has been inadvertently calling your number randomly at four P.M. This has been a computer error. We sincerely regret any inconvenience this has caused you and wish to assure you that the problem has been corrected. You will not be bothered again.

Sincerely yours,
The Phone Company

*   *   *

At dinner that night Maria suddenly said, "I've been thinking about my brother."

Her mother looked up sharply. Her father's jaw tightened.

"No, no," Maria said as lightly as she could. "The *new* one. The point is, we have to give him a name, right? What about — Toby? I've been practicing. Listen. 'This is my brother. My baby brother. His name is Toby. I'm teaching him to talk.' I'd say, 'Hello, Toby.' And then, you know, he'd say, 'Hello, Maria.'"

TEACHER TAMER

The whole fifth grade was engaged in silent reading. The students were reading their books while Mrs. Wessex, the teacher, sat at her desk in the front of the room, reading hers. Her book was a huge one titled *Crime and Punishment*. Fifteen minutes into the period, a large spitball landed on the middle of the page Mrs. Wessex was reading. She gasped — audibly.

As the class looked up, the teacher peered down at the page to see what had landed. When she lifted her face it was the color of chalk.

An uneasy murmur fluttered through the room.

Life in the fifth grade was never good when Mrs. Wessex was angry. Lately, her anger seemed to erupt daily. A tall, big-boned woman with large hands, she had graying, curly hair and wrinkles on her face. That day she was wearing a baggy blue dress that was also wrinkled.

"Nasty," was the way one student described her. No one disagreed.

She contemplated the class like a surgeon deciding where to cut. "Gregory Martinez!" she called. "Come here this instant!"

A hush fell upon the class as Gregory reluctantly slid out of his chair, then slumped to the front of the class, hands deep in his baggy pockets.

Gregory was short for his eleven years, and heavy-set. His complexion was dark, his hair black, his eyes intense and at the moment full of worry. Though he had been in the school only a few months, everyone at Kennedy Middle School knew he was a brain. When

Mrs. Wessex asked a question, it was always Gregory who had his hand up. More often than not he had the right answer, too.

Though Gregory liked being smart, his intelligence set him off from the other kids. He wanted to be liked, but they thought of him as different. Lately, however, things had begun to change.

During the past two weeks Mrs. Wessex had accused Gregory of various acts of misbehavior. She had gone so far as to punish him four times. Though getting into trouble improved Gregory's class standing, he kept insisting he was innocent. As far as he was concerned, Mrs. Wessex was picking on him. He wished he knew why.

Halfway to the teacher's desk, he said, "I didn't do it."

Mrs. Wessex stopped him in his tracks with a hard glare. "Didn't do *what*?" she demanded.

Instantly aware he had made a tactical mistake by saying anything before he was accused, he replied, "I was just reading."

"Come over here!" the teacher insisted. She pointed to a spot on the floor near her desk.

Gregory drew closer. Mrs. Wessex's desk was always neat. Its uncluttered state was taken by her slovenly students as a rebuke.

"Hands out of your pockets!" she snapped.

Gregory ripped his hands out, bringing a shower of small coins that scattered upon the floor. A burst of laughter erupted from thirty-six kids.

Trying desperately to keep from grinning, Gregory bent over to gather up the coins.

"Do that later!" Mrs. Wessex shouted. She had become angrier.

The classroom stilled instantly. Gregory felt his grin evaporate. As he tried to control his growing anxiety he stared at his feet.

"Do you see that?" the teacher demanded. She pointed right at her book. "Look!"

Gregory lifted his face. The spitball — surrounded by an expanding circle of moisture — lay upon the page. Not only did Gregory recognize the spitball for what it was, he knew that Ryan Jurgensen had shot it. Ryan, who occupied the desk right next to him, combined class bully, wiseass, and dummy in one skinny body topped with short-cropped blond hair. He was also school spitball artist, carrying a bundle of tissues and a bunch of large plastic straws in his pockets the way other kids carried pencils and erasers.

"*Do* you see that?" the teacher demanded of Gregory again.

"Yes, Mrs. Wessex."

"What is it?"

Gregory's dark face turned darker. "A — a spitball."

"Disgusting!" Mrs. Wessex informed him.

"I didn't do it," Gregory repeated with an intense sense of his own innocence.

"Young man, I believe you did!"

"I didn't!" Gregory protested.

"Then, who did?" she asked.

Gregory made a half turn toward the class. Though

he could sense other kids suppressing laughter at his plight, he felt they were on his side.

As for Ryan, not only did Gregory observe his barely stifled grin, he noted the bully's right fist balled up, a blatant threat that if Gregory dared to name him as culprit, the fist would be put to use.

"Gregory!" Mrs. Wessex said, "I asked you a question. If you didn't do this disgusting thing, who did?"

"I don't know," he replied, struggling to contain his sense of indignation. She had no right to blame him. "Mrs. Wessex," he suddenly blurted out, "how come you're always blaming me?"

The class gasped.

For a moment—but only a moment—Mrs. Wessex's face softened. Then she glared at him. "Gregory," she ordered, "go stand with your face in the shame corner for fifteen minutes."

"But I didn't do anything!" Gregory protested anew.

On appeal, Mrs. Wessex said, "Twenty minutes."

A giggle erupted from somewhere in the class.

"Quiet!" Mrs. Wessex cried.

Gregory, knowing that it would be useless to argue, shoved his hands back into his pockets and headed for the corner. Halfway there he stopped. "Mrs. Wessex, what about my money?"

"You may pick it up, then stand in the corner." This, from Mrs. Wessex, was a measure of kindness.

Hearing the suppressed snickers of his classmates, Gregory picked up the coins.

When he finally got into the shame corner, he was hot, upset, and angry. Mrs. Wessex was so unfair, he kept thinking. Staring into the corner, he vowed that this time he would have revenge.

During recess a bunch of kids gathered around him. "How come she picks on you?" Susan asked.

"I don't know," Gregory said, pleased that someone had noticed. "But I'm going to get back at her."

"Yeah, sure you will," Ryan teased. "Smartest kid

in class does something wicked to the teacher. Sure. Right."

Gregory looked at the circle of faces. His classmates were really paying attention to him. At the moment he felt they really liked him. If only he could do something to keep their positive feelings. "I *am* going to do something," he insisted.

"Everybody hear that?" Ryan crowed. "Gregory's going to get revenge on Wessex."

"Man," said Dori, "you do that you'll be the hero of the whole class."

Hero of the whole class. The words filled Gregory with excitement. He looked at Dori and smiled. Here was his opportunity. He would have his revenge and become a hero, too.

Two blocks from the Kennedy Memorial Middle School, tucked between Jack's Skate & Snow Boards and Robert's Famous Bar-Bee-Q-Ribs, stood Mrs. Barman's candy store. You could buy any piece of candy for five cents. During most of the day, the candy store had modest sales. Between the hours of three and four-thirty, it was packed with kids.

The display case contained fifty-two white plastic trays of candy, from Black Crows to clear jellybeans to white peppermints — and all colors and flavors in between.

Behind the display case stood Mrs. Barman. She was a small old woman whose marshmallow-colored face, arms, and torso seemed to be all there was of her. If she had a lower body, no one had ever seen it.

Kids asked for candy by pointing and saying "one" or "two." Mrs. Barman counted out the candy pieces and put them in a small white paper sack. "Fifteen cents," she'd say. The price was all she normally spoke.

It was to Mrs. Barman's that Gregory went after school. When it was his turn, the old lady gave him an inquiring look. "I want to speak to Tiny," Gregory announced.

Tiny was Mrs. Barman's son. If he was asked the proper way, he would sell you fireworks. Selling fireworks was illegal.

"Tiny!" Mrs. Barman shouted. "Kidtaseeya."

Gregory waited nervously. He had never spoken to Tiny before, and he was only remembering what some kid told him to do. He hoped he'd ask the right way. One of the things the kid had told him was, "You got to ask right, or Tiny won't sell you nothing."

Tiny, big as a grizzly bear, lumbered out of the backroom. He had a large, glistening bald head, an incredibly thick neck, and a belly so huge it was on the verge of splitting the plaid shirt he always wore. No one had ever seen him smile.

The kids had all kinds of stories about Tiny. Some said he had played professional football. Others said his size was due to the fact that he ate nothing but his mother's candy. Then there were those who claimed Mrs. Barman lost her bottom half because

Tiny had blown it away with his fireworks.

"Yawanme, kid?" Tiny said to Gregory. His voice was low, rumbling.

"Crackers," Gregory said, hoping he had remembered the password correctly.

Tiny looked hard at Gregory, then glanced around to make sure no fire marshal was lurking among the clamorous crowd of children.

"Follow me," he growled.

Gregory followed Tiny down a narrow, dark passageway into a small room whose walls were covered with metal drawers. A low-wattage bulb dangled from flimsy ceiling wires.

Gregory looked about. It was all so creepy he began to wish he hadn't come.

"Whadayawan?" Tiny asked.

Gregory, fist clenched, said, "A stink bomb and a smoke bomb."

Tiny studied Gregory anew. "Whacha goin'ta do wit'em?"

After a moment, Gregory said, "Put them in my teacher's house."

Tiny's face unfolded into a smile. "I hate teachas," he said. The smile vanished. "Seventy-five cent each," he said.

Gregory laboriously counted out the quarters, nickels, dimes, and pennies into Tiny's huge hands.

"An' twenty-five cent," Tiny added. "Fa-da guvament tax."

Gregory handed over the surcharge.

The large man opened two metal drawers and extracted two small tubes, each as thick as his thumbs. Frizzy gray fuses protruded from their ends. One tube was black and bore a label that read SUPER SKUNK. The other tube was a bright orange color and was called CLOUD OF DARKNESS.

"Okay, kid," Tiny said, "where'dya get tha stuff?"

Gregory struggled to recall the proper reply. "Some kid," he said.

"Don'cha forget," Tiny said. Turning Gregory around

with his big hands, he pushed him out of the room. But not before he whispered, "Go getcha teacha."

Gregory left the candy store at a trot and went right to a gas station down the block. It sold cookies, chips, and soda. He went in and made a show of looking at the offerings. When no one was looking, he grabbed a book of complimentary matches from the counter and raced back to school.

At four-thirty Mrs. Wessex stepped out of the school. In each hand she had a cloth shopping bag loaded with books and papers. One bag bore the faded words, If You Can Read This Thank a Teacher.

Gregory, crouched behind a parked car across the street, was waiting and watching for her.

He found it easy to follow her. Not only was Mrs. Wessex a large woman, she was wearing a bright blue coat. Though Gregory knew — without knowing how he knew — that she lived in that neighborhood, he didn't know where. But then, he still didn't know his way around the area very well. In any case, she

walked slowly. To Gregory it appeared she had no
interest other than in the pavement before her.

When she went into a small grocery store, Gregory
hid behind a garbage can. Emerging, she carried a
paper bag stuffed with goods. Every now and then
she paused and clumsily shifted her load. She was
having trouble balancing all her belongings.

Gregory, clutching his stink and smoke bombs in
his pocket, followed at a safe distance. At one point he
thought she might be turning to look. He quickly
ducked behind some passing people. When the
teacher continued on without looking back, so did
Gregory. He was becoming excited.

One block from the grocery store, Mrs. Wessex
made a right turn onto Pearl Street, an old street bor-
dered by large oak trees. The early spring leaves were
bright green. Pearl Street ran through a dilapidated
neighborhood of small wooden houses. Gregory had
never been on the street before. Potholes marred the
pavement. Many of the houses, if not quite in a state

of decay, were in need of new paint and carpentry. Porches sagged. Paint peeled. Here and there a cracked window winked at the world.

After walking another six blocks, Mrs. Wessex turned onto a cement pathway that led to one of the single-story frame houses. It was in a row of similar houses. All had small porches. The house Mrs. Wessex entered was set back from the street by a small, sparse lawn and was covered with dull white aluminum siding. Two cracked cement steps led up to the front porch. Beyond the porch was a faded yellow door.

Upon reaching the porch, Mrs. Wessex set down her two shopping bags, shifted the paper bag, and entered the house. In moments she returned, gathered up the shopping bags, then went back inside again. This time she shut the door firmly behind her.

Gregory, standing behind a lamppost, had watched her intently. Only when Mrs. Wessex had gone in did he appraise the house. The building's rundown appearance was not what he had expected. He was not sure why, but he had assumed his teacher was rich. The apartment house he lived in was in better condition.

And now that he'd actually arrived at Mrs. Wessex's house, Gregory began to feel uneasy. What if she had kids? What if there was a *Mr.* Wessex? What if he got caught? Worst of all, what if he did nothing, and the kids at school got on his case? Instead of being a hero, he'd be more of a nerd than ever. He wished he'd not been so public about proclaiming his revenge. He remembered Ryan's taunt, Dori's promise. He squeezed the smoke and stink bombs in his pocket, then touched the book of matches. He had to go on.

Mrs. Wessex's house was no more than five feet from the homes to the right and left. In the alleyway between her house and the one on the right was a jungle of bushes. As far as Gregory could tell, that side of the house had no windows. Then he saw what appeared to be a window low to the ground. Partly open, it was built into the building's foundation.

Gregory guessed it led into the basement.

After making sure no one was watching him, Gregory darted across the street and into the tangle of greenery. Once there he threaded his way through the foliage to the low window and squatted down. To his surprise, Mrs. Wessex's house was propped up by cement block pillars. Between the pillars was siding. There was no basement. What he had thought was a window was nothing more than a sheet of wood, which covered a gap in the siding.

Gregory touched the board. It fell over with a loud thump. Fearful of discovery, he darted a look over his shoulder. No one was coming.

Feeling safe again, he peered through the gaping hole into a crawlspace.

Next door someone stepped out onto the porch, slamming the front door. Fearful of discovery, Gregory dove into the crawlspace beneath Mrs. Wessex's house. There he lay, face down on the dirt, breathing hard. His courage was evaporating.

When no further sounds came from next door, Gregory lifted his head and looked about. It was gloomy there with a strong, clammy stench that almost made him throw up. Fumbling, Gregory drew out his pack of matches and lit one. The area from the ground to the house was no more than three feet in height. It was littered with junk: bottles, cans, clumps of matted newspapers, an old mattress, even a broken birdcage. Overhead ran crisscrossing pipes and wires. So unlike Mrs. Wessex's desk!

Even as Gregory looked about he heard footsteps above his head. Automatically, he ducked. The match went out.

Gregory listened intently. He heard the sound of muffled voices, but who was speaking, or what was being said, he couldn't tell.

The footsteps retreated. The voices drifted away.

He lifted his head. The more he looked around the more perfect the crawlspace seemed as a place to set off the bombs. All he had to do was find the right location so that stink and smoke would get into the house. His courage returned. He touched the bombs and grinned.

Lit match in hand, he explored the area by crawling around. It took three more matches to discover something promising. A trap door. At least it was a square over his head with hinges on one side and a metal latch opposite.

Gregory worked his way beneath the door, then lit another match and examined the latch. It was a metal shot bolt. He yanked at it. Not only did it pull free, the door dropped down, smacking him hard on his head. Gregory saw stars.

When he recovered, he looked about. Three shoes had fallen to the ground. After pushing them aside, he crawled directly under the now open space. Another lit match allowed him to look up.

At first it seemed as if he were gazing up into a bundle of rags.

The match went out.

Gregory drew himself up on his knees, then slowly lifted his head until it was poking up through the opening. He was inside the house. The area was quite dark save for one side where, along the floor, ran a strip of light. Gregory guessed he was seeing room light seeping under a door. That made him realize where he was: in a clothes closet. Better and better.

He decided to take a chance and light one more match. The flame revealed clothing hung from wire and plastic hangers on two sides of the closet. Against another wall — all in a heap — lay shoes and slippers. On the fourth wall was a door. There was also a plastic basket heaped with rumpled clothing. High above was shelving holding a variety of boxes. In the ceiling was an unlit bulb.

Hearing nothing, Gregory pulled himself up until he was standing in the dark closet. Reaching into his pocket, he pulled out the stink and smoke bombs. He made up his mind to light them, jerk the door open, heave the bombs in, then make his escape.

He'd even be able to watch what happened from out front.

He took out the matches.

Suddenly, he heard a voice from beyond the closet.

". . . tell you how exhausted I am. I have to lie down."

It was Mrs. Wessex.

"You're always complaining," said another voice. To Gregory's ears it sounded like an older woman, but he could not be sure.

"I'm not complaining," Mrs. Wessex said.

Gregory's first impulse was to dive back down the hole and make his escape. His second impulse was to stay and listen. He was in his teacher's closet! Listening to her *private* stuff. *Irresistible.* He leaned forward and put his ear to the door.

"My dear," said the voice of the older woman, "I just wish you wouldn't come home from that school so tired every day."

"Ma, it is exhausting, that's all. I just need to lie down."

"Well, you could be thankful you have a good job. Lots of people don't have one."

Suddenly the closet doorknob rattled. Panicked, Gregory flung himself to one side. The door opened. The closet seemed to explode with light. The blue dress Mrs. Wessex had worn that day came flying through the open door and fell in a heap on the floor. It was followed by a pink bra. The door slammed shut.

Gregory looked at the clothes and nearly fainted. What was he doing there! He had done a terrible thing. He'd be arrested. Put in jail! He lowered his feet into the trap door.

"Ma . . . ," the voice continued from beyond.

"Madge, try to remember they're just children. And you do get vacations."

"Ma, I've been teaching for fifteen years. I have thirty-six kids in my class. I get lousy pay. Each year the kids get worse and worse. Ruder and ruder. They don't want to learn. All they can talk about is sports, movies, and TV. They can't even sit still. They hate me."

"Sometimes I think you should have stayed married to Benny. You could have had your own kids."

"Do you know what happened today?"

"Benny wasn't such a bad man, Madge. Yeah, he drank a little. But really, not much. And when he was transferred — "

"Ma, listen to me! Today, I was sitting there reading. It was reading time. Someone shot a spitball right on my book."

"A what?"

"A spitball."

"That's dreadful. Can't your principal do something?"

"Ma, you don't understand."

"Madge, I'm trying to understand."

"You don't understand!" cried Mrs. Wessex. "I knew who did it. Ryan Jurgensen. The class clown. But he thrives on being the center of attention.

So instead, I called up this boy . . . Gregory. . . ."

"Why him?"

"Because Gregory is the smartest one in the class. It makes the other kids resent him. But I keep thinking if I pick on him enough the other kids will accept him. Can you grasp that? I'm afraid that if the kids turn against him, he'll want to deny his intelligence. I want to keep him smart. That's what it comes to. I'm picking on him so he'll stay smart and amount to something. It's crazy.

"But you know what, Ma? At the same time I resent Gregory. Because he's so young and could do so much and I can't do anything anymore."

"What did he do when you blamed him?"

"Gregory? He made fun of me."

"How?"

"He dumped his money—coins—on the floor."

"Please, Madge, I wish you wouldn't cry."

"Ma, do you know what it is like to have a room full of kids who hate you, despise you, have no respect for you? I hate teaching. I used to be good. I can't stand it anymore."

"You've had a bad day, that's all. Or maybe you should think about getting another position."

"Sure. And if I can't get one, what are we supposed to live on? Your social security?"

"Go to sleep, honey. You're tired. You'll feel better when you're rested."

There was silence.

In the closet, Gregory, who had heard it all, pressed a hand to his heart to keep it from beating so wildly.

He listened and thought he detected the sounds of someone outside the closet. Was it Mrs. Wessex on her bed? He kept listening. After a while, he began to hear snores. Mrs. Wessex's *snores*! He started to laugh, but the laugh faded. He thought of what he had heard, and all he could feel was a heaviness in his heart.

Quietly, he lowered himself the rest of the way through the trap door. Once in the crawlspace, he looked around for the shoes that had fallen down. He put them back into the closet with care, then shut the trap door and latched it. When he made his way out from under the house, he ran all the way home, dumping the firecrackers in a garbage can.

The next morning Gregory was waiting at the school before they let the early arrivals into the building. He was glad none of the kids from his class were there.

As soon as the doors were unlocked, he raced down the hallway toward his classroom. He reached it. Mrs. Wessex was alone in the room. She was at her desk, working on papers.

Gregory edged into the room.

After a moment Mrs. Wessex looked up. She began to smile, caught herself, and frowned. "Yes, Gregory," she said, rather severely. "The bell hasn't rung. What do you want?"

In spite of himself, Gregory blushed. "It was about yesterday."

"Yes . . . ?" said Mrs. Wessex. There was pain in her eyes.

Gregory wanted to put his arms around her and give her a hug. Instead he said, "I just wanted to say . . . you're the best teacher in . . . the . . . the whole world."

A startled look came to Mrs. Wessex's face. For a moment Gregory thought she was going to cry. "Why do you say that?" she asked.

"I just think so." He looked down at his feet.

"Oh . . . ," she said, very softly. "Thank you."

On the playground, his classmates gathered around.

"Did you get your revenge?" Ryan taunted.

"Yeah," Gregory replied.

"Cool. What did you do?"

"Never mind what. Just see the way she acts."

Gregory was right. It was almost a month before Mrs. Wessex became angry again.

But not before Ryan had given him a new name: "Teacher Tamer."

PETS

Eve Hubbard had a passion for pets. Her entire life had been filled with gerbils, hamsters, a rat, turtles, a dog, a salamander, and most recently, cats.

In the beginning there was Chase. He was the dog Eve's parents got before she was born. A dalmatian, his original name was Clark, but Eve so loved the way he chased other animals, squirrels, birds, cats, other dogs, that she changed his name to Chase.

When Chase died of old age, Eve was very sad. She insisted they bury him in their backyard. This yard was enclosed by a high brick wall, crowded with trees, shrubs, and flowers. It was a shady, often damp place, where the moss grew thick, while strange-looking mushrooms sprang up overnight, and withered and died just as quickly.

Midgarden was a small, murky pool in which, during the summer, fat goldfish swam. As they darted about the dark water, Eve was reminded of summer heat lightning.

It was in this yard that Chase was laid to rest with a large stone to mark the spot.

Eve's parents decided against another dog. But though her young brother, Jeff, was uninterested in animals, Eve was allowed to have many other pets. None seemed to survive for very long. When they died Eve buried them in the backyard, too. In time there was quite a row of stones, even a cluster of pebbles for departed goldfish.

Most recently Eve came to have two kittens. When she got them she made a vow that these pets would survive. One was white with blue eyes and a pink nose. She named her Angel. The black one — a male with yellow eyes and black nose — she called Shadow.

Eve lavished so much care and affection on Angel and Shadow that she was quite certain she loved these pets more than the others. She was equally sure they loved her just as much. There was nothing she would not do for them. She fed them. Washed and groomed them. Talked to them. Petted them. Not only did they thrive, they grew to maturity.

But there were some problems with Angel.

Early on, the two cats had learned that their food was offered at five o'clock. Twenty minutes before the hour, the two could always be found sitting by their bowls, tails twitching as they waited impatiently for Eve to feed them. If Eve was tardy, Angel scolded her loudly. Once, when Eve was twenty minutes late, Angel nipped Eve's hand as their bowls were being filled. That, despite an apology from Eve.

The cats had another eating habit that Eve

attributed to a kind of "ladies first" politeness. That is, Shadow always waited for Angel to start before he began to eat.

Once—just as an experiment—Eve held Angel back in order to let Shadow eat first. A furious Angel scratched Eve and butted Shadow aside.

"I promise I won't do that again," Eve said, sucking the blood from her hand.

Then there was the time Eve purchased a catnip mouse for the cats. It was a Christmas present she bought with her own money. Instead of sharing it, Angel took the stuffed creature into a corner. When Shadow tried to get at it, Angel hissed. Eve—wanting them to share—took the toy away from her and gave it to Shadow.

That night, when Eve was going down the steps, Angel got between her legs. If Eve hadn't managed to grab the banister, she would have fallen. It was almost as if Angel had wanted Eve to hurt herself.

Now and again, Angel caught one of the goldfish

in the garden pool. Not that she ate any of them. Instead, she left them by the edge of the pool, as if to warn the other goldfish of her prowess. And twice — when Eve had scolded her about bullying Shadow — she'd carried a dead goldfish into the house and left it on Eve's pillow.

Eve, in her great love for the cats, forgave these excesses.

One late summer day Angel grew ill. She stopped eating, became thin as a rail, developed a dry nose and runny eyes, and mewed continually, as though asking Eve to *do* something. Despite the special food Eve prepared, despite her tending to Angel every free moment, the cat's legs grew shaky. Her fur, once thick and velvet in its brushed and combed lushness, became scruffy and unkempt.

"I'm afraid it's feline distemper," the veterinarian said in his examining room with the stainless steel tabletop. "I'm sorry to say your friend won't recover.

My dear, I think we should put her out of her misery."
He looked from Eve to her father. "One injection will
do. I promise she won't feel the least bit of pain. As it
is, your other cat might catch the same disease. Even
humans do, sometimes. What's your cat's name?"

"Angel."

"I am sorry," he said, and sounded sincere.

Tears trickled from Eve's eyes. There was no arguing with what she could see for herself.

Though the vet — and her father — advised against
it, Eve insisted on holding Angel in her arms when
the fatal injection was administered. "You don't know
how much we love each other," Eve explained softly.

Angel died quickly and painlessly in Eve's arms,
with barely a sound, save for one long, soft hiss and
a frightful last look that Eve interpreted as meaning,
"Why have you done this to me?"

The vet — citing local law — said Angel could not
be buried in Eve's backyard.

As if all that was not heartbreaking enough,

when Eve returned home she felt compelled to explain to Shadow what had happened.

"No more parties for Angel," she told Shadow. "No more dressing her up and pushing her in the baby carriage or pretending she's queen of the house and we, her loyal servants. Oh, Shadow, she's gone. Forever."

Eve's mother offered the gentle suggestion that perhaps Shadow would not understand what had happened to Angel. Indignantly, Eve replied that she was old enough to know her own as well as her cat's mind. "Shadow *will* understand," she insisted. "And nobody loves her pets so well as I do," she said, midst hot tears.

Within twenty-four hours Eve began to wonder if her mother was right concerning Shadow's capacity to understand. He became edgy and acted strangely. He spent hours searching for the dead Angel. Not only did Shadow keep making the rounds of the white cat's particular haunts, he kept returning to her favorite sleeping spot, the orange seat on the old wing chair in the dark corner of the living room. Though Shadow himself preferred the couch throw pillow, after Angel's death he spent most of his sleeping hours near her spot.

Shadow even had to be encouraged to eat. It was as if he could not accept the notion that Angel was not going to return and feared she would not like it if he ate first.

Two weeks after Angel's death, in the middle of the night, a noise woke Eve. She was in her bed, on the second floor of her house, beneath a feather comforter, with her body snug and warm, her face open to the crisp air. What was it, she wondered, that had woken her? Was it the cry of a cat?

In her drowsy state it took her a moment to remember that Angel had died. Usually, the cats lay at the foot of her bed, more often than not with Angel using Shadow as a pillow.

Eve felt about with her toes. There were no cats on her bed. She sat up and looked on the floor.

Shadow was not there, either. Troubled, Eve swung

her feet out from under the comforter and walked to the door of her room.

"Shadow!" she called softly.

When there was no reply she called again, louder.

Eve went to the window of her room and looked into the backyard. The night sky was lit up by a three-quarter moon of great brightness. Only a few clouds — like knots of darkness — drifted by. Because of the moonlight, few stars were visible. But there was Shadow, sitting by the edge of the goldfish pool, staring up.

"Shadow!" Eve called.

The black cat looked at Eve but — as though summoned — quickly shifted his gaze back to whatever it was that was attracting his attention.

Eve padded downstairs. At the base of the steps she paused to listen. Her parents — she was quite certain — were asleep. So, presumably, was her younger brother, Jeff.

Eve went out the back door, which was open when

it should have been closed. Though the cement patio was cold to her bare feet, she continued on.

It took Eve a moment to adjust her eyes to the backyard's gloom, but when she searched about she saw Shadow gazing up just as she had seen him from above. The fur along his black back was standing up. His tail was fluffed out. Eve could see right away that he was very frightened. "Shadow!" Eve whispered. "What is it?"

The black cat swished his tail but did not alter his gaze. Puzzled, Eve sat down on the ground and put her head next to Shadow's head — the better to follow his look — and searched again.

In the tree — out along a branch — was a white cat. "Angel!" Eve cried.

The white cat hissed and vanished.

Shaken, Eve gathered Shadow in her arms and pressed her face into his thick, sweet-smelling neck. The black cat was trembling.

Eve carried Shadow back to her room and placed

him gently on his accustomed sleeping spot at the foot of her bed. The cat flexed his back, walked a tight circle—as if to unwind himself—kneaded the comforter, then plopped down. But he slept, not by Eve's feet, but close to her hands.

"Can animals become ghosts?" Eve asked at the breakfast table the next morning.

Her father lowered his newspaper. "What?"

"When an animal dies, can it become a ghost?"

"What kind of animal?" Jeff asked between mouthfuls of Corn Pops and milk. Jeff was seven.

Eve gave her younger brother a disdainful glance. "Can animals become ghosts?" she asked again.

Her mother, who was reading another part of the newspaper, said, "You have to believe in ghosts first."

"Guess what," Jeff interrupted.

"What?"

"Animals can't be ghosts."

Eve looked across the room. Shadow was sitting atop the counter, yellow eyes fixed on her. Eve had no doubt he was paying attention to the conversation.

"Shadow believes in ghosts," Eve informed her brother and anyone else who might be listening. "So there," she said and left for school.

In school Eve went to the library and requested a book about ghosts.

"A ghost story?" the librarian asked.

"Not really," Eve explained. "I need to find out some facts about them. What they are. What they want. You see I have one. An animal one."

The librarian looked a little queerly at Eve. But all she said was, "Let me show you what we have." She found a book for Eve titled *The Truth About Ghosts.*

"Cool," Eve said, and worked her way through the pages. What she learned was that ghosts — if you believed in them — came back to haunt the living because during the ghosts' lives something had been left incomplete, undone, or unsaid. Perhaps they could not bear to be apart from those still living. Or they wanted something they could not get where they were.

From the time the cats had been kittens, Eve had tried to train them to lay upon her chest so they could talk out the day before going to sleep. Cats, she knew perfectly well, did not talk. But she was willing to translate their looks into speech. Angel had always refused, but Shadow was willing.

So that evening he sat on her chest, black nose just a few inches from Eve's nose, staring at her with his large yellow eyes and purring like an idling motor.

"Why do you think Angel has come back?" Eve asked. Shadow yawned and turned away.

"Shadow," said Eve, "I think she's haunting you."

"I want you to promise me something," Eve continued. "If you step out to see Angel's ghost again, let me know so I can go with you and tell her to leave you alone. Okay?"

Shadow blinked.

It was two in the morning when Eve woke. Shadow wasn't there. The door was open.

Eve hurried down the steps and into the yard. The

moon was bright enough that she could spot Shadow at the edge of the pool, staring into a tree. Angel was in the tree.

"What is it, Angel?" she called gently. "What's the matter? Why can't you rest? What do you want?"

Amid the dark leaves, Angel's body seemed to be shining. Her tail jerked about angrily. Her glare was hostile.

Eve felt something prickly against her leg. Startled, she looked down. It was Shadow, cringing behind her.

"I want you to know," Eve informed Angel with some indignation, "you are scaring Shadow."

The white cat vanished.

The following day Shadow grew sluggish. That evening he did not eat his dinner.

"Shadow," said Eve during their bedtime conversation, "Angel can be very insistent. Remember that time with the catnip mouse?

"You didn't eat tonight," Eve continued. "That's the way Angel's sickness began. I think you're going to get sick, and die, and go to her. I believe she wants you where she is so she can have someone to sleep on. Do you think that's so? How can I help you stay?" she asked tearfully. "I'll do anything."

Shadow, his front paws tucked rather primly under his chest, gazed evenly at Eve with his round yellow eyes. He licked one of his paws and passed the wet paw over his face, as if wiping away tears. Then he got up and walked slowly to the foot of Eve's bed. Instead of doing his usual turn and settling down for the night, he jumped off the bed and crept out of the room, belly low.

"Don't listen to her!" Eve called after him. "Don't!"

She went to the window. The moon was close to being full. As she watched, she saw Shadow walk into the garden and take up his position by the goldfish pond. He was staring into the tree. Eve glanced at the stone that marked Chase's burial spot — and all the other animals' markers — and decided not to go down.

Over the next few days Shadow's health grew

worse. Signs of distemper were unmistakable. This time, however, Eve didn't wait quite so long before asking her mother to take the cat to the veterinarian.

He set Shadow on the stainless steel examination table and felt around his ears, looked into his mouth, took his temperature.

"It's what I was afraid of," the vet said sadly, once he had concluded his examination. "He must have gotten the illness from your other cat.

"But cats," the vet warned, "are a bit like people in regard to illness. Living or dying—it can have a lot to do with what they want. Has this fellow been grieving for his partner?"

"He's being haunted by her," Eve said solemnly.

The vet exchanged glances with Eve's mother. To Eve, he said, "Happens that way with humans too, sometimes. Let's hope you caught this illness early enough," he said soothingly and offered Eve a packet of pink pills, as well as instructions on how to give them to Shadow. "Call me if he gets worse."

That night Eve tried talking to Shadow again. His yellow eyes were dull. His nose was dry. "Please tell me what I can do to help you resist Angel," she said to him. "It's not our fault she died. It's not right that she wants to take you with her."

When Shadow made no response, Eve became almost angry. "Shadow," she said, "who picked you out at the ASPCA? Who always fed you and brushed you? Had birthday parties and Christmas with you? Who talks to you every night? Listens to you, lets you sleep on her bed? Please don't forget any of that. *Please.*"

Shadow shut his eyes.

"Oh, Shadow!" Eve cried in frustration. "It's not fair!"

Over the next few days Shadow grew more ill despite the fact that Eve gave him the pills the way the vet had instructed her. She pried the black cat's mouth open, popped a pill deep into his pink throat, then gently held his mouth closed so that he had to swallow.

It was only later that she found a pile of the pink pills — spit up — behind the wing chair. Eve feared there was nothing more she could do. Angel had insisted Shadow join her. And he was going.

Even so, Eve kept trying to convince Shadow to stay. She spoke to him about the pleasures of life in their house, with her, the family. "We all love you," she said. Shadow merely listened.

"I'll get you a new friend," Eve pleaded. "I'll go to the ASPCA and find someone this weekend. I'll even look for a white one. A white kitten would be so much fun. Oh, Shadow," she cried, holding the now thin creature close to her heart, "don't go to Angel. Stay with me."

Though he grew sicker, Shadow went out each night and looked up at the tree. Eve, tears running down her cheeks, watched him from her room. How could Angel be so powerful?

"I'm afraid he's doing just as poorly as Angel," Eve's father said Saturday morning.

"He doesn't want to live," Eve informed him.

"You mean, he misses Angel?"

"Dad," Eve said with some bitterness, "Angel is *insisting* he join her. And Shadow always does what she tells him to do."

"My suggestion," her father said, "is that we take him back to the vet."

That night, when Shadow dragged himself out into the garden, Eve joined him. The black cat sat by the pool, occasionally looking up. Often, in his weakness, he nodded off.

The white cat was in the tree.

"Angel," said Eve, "why must you do this? It wasn't our fault you died. Just because you died doesn't mean everybody else has to. Shadow has a right to his life."

The white cat opened her mouth and hissed.

"And what about me?" Eve cried. "Don't you care about how I feel?"

Angel hissed again.

The next morning Eve and her mother took Shadow to the vet. It was of no use. Shadow died the way Angel had—in Eve's arms.

On the way home, Eve was very silent. All she could think about was that Angel had betrayed her. She was hurt and very angry.

Eve's mother reached out and touched her. "When you're ready you can get another cat."

Eve said nothing. But she kept asking herself, why was Angel treating her so badly? Had she done something wrong? Had she offended the cats in some way? No, she insisted to herself. It was just the opposite. She had loved them. Given them so much.

The next day a sad Eve put away the cats' bowls, cleaned and stored their litter box, shelved the remaining cans of cat food, and put the cats' collars in a box of mementos she kept at the back of her closet. Her sleep was uninterrupted.

Then, two nights after Shadow died, Eve woke. She

turned on her reading lamp and looked toward her feet. Both dead cats, Angel and Shadow, were looking at her, staring with unblinking eyes.

Eve was so shocked she drew in her breath sharply. She hardly knew what to do other than to stare back. Suddenly it dawned on her why the cats were there. "Oh, Shadow, oh Angel," she cried. "You've come back for *me*, haven't you? You want me to be with you."

The cats stared fixedly at her.

"But why do you want me?" Eve asked. "Is it because you love me so much?"

Eve sat up in bed — arms hugged around her knees — gazing at the cats, waiting for a response. They made not so much as a sound.

After a while Angel stood, arched her back, and crept forward. Approaching Eve, she leaned down and bit her hand.

"Ow!" Eve cried, snatching her hand away. She sucked at the blood.

Angel sat back on her haunches, licked her lips, and stared at Eve.

Eve suddenly remembered that what Angel did was exactly what she had done that time she thought her food was late. Then, all in rush, Eve understood.

"Is that all I am to you?" she gasped with horror. "Just someone to take care of you? Your servant. Your *pet*?"

The cats vanished.

The next day Eve told no one of the cats' visit. They didn't believe her before. She knew they wouldn't believe her now. Besides, she was sure she was strong. She would be able to resist the cats' demands.

Four days later the two cats returned. They called to her — soft, plaintive mewing sounds — in her sleep. When she woke she knew they were in the yard.

It was a warm, humid night, the last hot breath of the summer that had been. When Eve stepped onto the patio, she felt almost suffocated by the fragrance that filled the air, the thick, clotted scent of decaying vegetation. The limp leaves on the trees were edged with brown. A heavy dew clung to the plants and shrubbery and weighed them down. Rotting mushrooms glowed faintly and seemed to pulse. A waning moon slipped in and out behind streaks of clouds. In the pool floated a dead goldfish. Its white belly was turned up, a mirror image to the moon in the sky.

The two cats were sitting side by side beneath the tree. Angel seemed to be in bloom. Shadow's ebony fur shimmered. Their tails waved with impatience.

Before the cats were their food bowls. The bowls were empty. Eve understood instantly. The cats were waiting for her to feed them.

Eve stamped her foot. "No," she said. "I will not take care of you anymore. I won't. And there's nothing you can do to make me!"

The cats meowed with aggravation, but faded away.

Over the next few days Eve suffered various visitations. The cats hissed in dark rooms, swiped at her as she went down the hallway. A bleeding scratch appeared on the back of her hand. She tripped over *something* as she came down the steps. A dead gold-fish lay on her pillow. It stank badly.

"I'm not going to join you," Eve told the cats when she saw them next.

Angel spat at her.

Shadow had the decency to look away.

At dinner the following day, Eve said, "I have an important announcement."

Her mother, father, and brother looked at her.

"The cats," said Eve, "have come back as ghosts. They are trying to get me to join them."

"Oh yeah, why?" her brother demanded.

"So I can take care of them."

"But they're dead!" her brother protested.

"I just told you, it's their ghosts!"

Eve's mother and father exchanged bemused looks.

"Well," her mother said, "I know they were attached to you."

"And you to them," her father added.

"You think I'm joking, don't you?" said Eve. She left the table sorry she had spoken to them.

The following day Eve became ill. First came fatigue, aching joints, sore throat — then a fever.

Both of Eve's parents worked, so a baby-sitter had to be brought in to stay with the ailing girl. It was on the third day, when Eve's fever grew high, that Eve's father remained home. When he went to work her mother came home. When his school was out, Jeff sat with her. Eve, however, had eyes for only Angel and Shadow, who either sat or slept at the foot of her bed. They kept gazing at her, mewing, waving their tails. Eve knew they were only waiting for her to die and come take care of them.

"I'm not your pet," she said to them vehemently. "I'm staying here."

"Daddy," she begged, "make them go away."

Her father got a cold compress and laid it over her forehead. "This should help your fever," he said gently.

After the fourth day of high fever, Eve was taken to the hospital. The cats followed her to the sterile white room that almost put Angel's coat to shame. As for Shadow, he looked like a dirty oil spill at the foot of the bed, where they were sitting.

Once, when Eve woke from a deep sleep, she found both cats sitting on her chest. They were side by side, pink and black noses two inches from her face.

"Take care of yourselves!" she cried out angrily. With that she fell into a faint.

That night she was sent home. Her parents and her brother were beside her. They looked sad and whispered among themselves. Sometimes there were tears.

At the foot of the bed, the two cats, paws folded under their chests, waited patiently.

"Please make the cats go away," Eve said, feebly.

Her family, seeing nothing, could only shake their heads.

That night Eve woke at about two in the morning. Feverish and weak, she crawled out of bed and went to the window. Leaning against the window frame for support, she peered down into the yard. The two cats were there, waiting by their empty bowls. They looked up at Eve and mewed.

A wave of exhaustion washed over the girl. "They need me," she told herself. "They must be very hungry. It must be time to feed them. Only I can do it."

She gazed about the yard until her eyes came to rest on Chase's grave. In the moonlight his marker stone was radiant. Where was he? Why had *he* never come back to haunt her? Presumably he lay in peace. Eve envied the dog.

With a sigh of resignation, she took up her robe, wrapped it around herself, and went slowly downstairs and into the yard.

Though the night air made her shiver, her forehead felt as if it were burning. Her body was so hot she was sweating. As soon as the cats saw her, they began to mew angrily and swish their tails as if they were whips.

Then a thought came to her. Eve stumbled past the cats and into the yard to the area where all her pets had been buried.

The cats, complaining bitterly, darted between her feet, clawing her ankles, nipping at her.

At Chase's grave Eve sank to her knees.

Shadow bit her bare toes. Angel clawed her ankle.

Eve was too far gone to notice these attacks. "Chase," she whispered in a trembling voice, "please come back. I need you badly. I want you to chase these cats away."

So saying, she squeezed her hands together and repeated her words passionately.

Suddenly there was a bark. Eve looked around. It was dim, her vision was fogged, but there before her — unmistakably — was Chase. In her delirium Eve saw him in reverse: where he had been white, he was now black, and his black spots were now white.

Chase paid no attention to her, but was galloping madly toward the cats. Behind him followed a ragged parade of salamanders, turtles, hamsters, gerbils, and many flopping goldfish. All were ghosts.

The cats spun about, hissed, and spat, but as Chase approached, they gave ground quickly. They ran for the wall, scampered up, and disappeared over the top. Chase, panting, stood at the base of the wall and barked furiously. The other ghosts made appropriate noises.

When the cats were gone, Chase trotted over to where Eve was, barked once, twice, then evaporated.

Eve barely made it back to her bed.

But starting the next morning, she became better. Every day that followed she improved, until the doctor declared her cured. He was even heard to say, "And I didn't think she had a ghost of a chance."

In the years that followed, on the anniversary of Chase's death, Eve never failed to leave a large dog biscuit on his burial stone. During that particular night—she always waited up to hear—there invariably was a bark. And in the morning the biscuit was gone.

As for pets, Eve never wanted another.

WHAT'S INSIDE

That fall term we seventh graders had a choice of electives: art, music, or woodworking. You had to take each of them during the course of the year but you could usually pick the order in which you took them.

I asked for woodworking because I always liked fooling around with tools. We had some in our basement, and I was allowed to bang about with them as long as I didn't break anything.

The first time the class met, Mr. Hanks — the shop teacher — said we could make what we wanted, but the first and only thing we were required to make was a square box. He showed us one he had made.

There was a general groan. Like, not cool. Know what I'm saying? A box seemed so *nerdy*. Talk about square. I thought, what can you do with a box— except put something in it?

Turned out, a box—if you're going to make it right—is a wicked hard thing to do. See, you have to cut every piece *precisely* the same size; and when you cut the pieces, each one has to be *exactly* square. 'Cause when you put it together they have to fit exactly right. Otherwise it's lopsided, weird looking, like that old shoebox you keep your busted—but decent—sneakers in.

Finally, when you put a hinged lid on this box— another requirement—that made it even harder. It had to close absolutely.

To show how it was done right, Mr. Hanks put a turned-on flashlight in his box, closed the lid, and switched off the shop lights. Everything was pitch dark. No light leaked out from his box. He said, "If I see any light oozing from your box, you'll have to fix it."

"What if I don't put any light inside?" someone shouted out.

We laughed. Mr. Hanks, grinning, said, "If you want to get out of this class alive, my friend, you better have *something* inside that box. And I better not see it."

It took me four weeks of classes—and a lot of after-school hours—but when my box was done—stained, varnished, waxed—not only had I learned a whole lot, it looked pretty sweet. And no light leaked out. You could have put a million bucks in that sucker. Or nothing. No one would have seen the difference.

When I took the box home, my parents went on about it so much—how neat, beautiful, and useful it was—I decided to make a second box and give one to each of them for Christmas presents. You know, His and Her boxes. So what if you couldn't tell them apart? Pretty neat, I thought.

That's just what I did, and Christmas morning my folks were real happy. In fact, Christmas afternoon, during the annual big family Christmas party, which was at my house that year, my parents put them on display. That made me feel good, though I acted, you know, cool. Like, you don't want people to know what you're feeling, right?

It was during that same afternoon — my cousin Danny saw the boxes.

Danny was fifteen — two years older than me — a big geeky guy, always bumping into things, knocking stuff over, like he was trying to get through the dark. The kid couldn't walk into a room without slamming into something, after which his pimply pizza face turned tomato red. And he usually spoke only apologies. I mean he was the type who if you gave him a birthday present, would have apologized for being born.

When he did say something it was mostly sad and distant. For example, I once said — sincerely — "Hey, man, that's a cool shirt." And he said, "My folks made me wear it." Know what I'm saying? The guy was so down, if he climbed out of his hole, he'd still be in the basement—and the lights would be off.

Most times he kept to himself and just hung around, watching with those mournful eyes of his. I never saw him smile much, or even straighten up.

His parents were not much happier. At the moment, his mother—my father's sister—worked at a Burger King, while his dad did local trucking. I don't know, from what I heard my parents say, their life seemed always to be crashing into holes. One crisis after another. Nothing was ever right. Things were always getting tangled. They were their own three-person traffic jam.

Now the point is, one of the weird things about Danny was that he seemed to like me. I didn't know why. But I have to admit, I was sort of flattered. He was already in high school. But no way cool, so it was a little embarrassing, too.

Anyway, that Christmas afternoon, there he was staring at those boxes, opening and closing their lids, measuring just how big their insides were.

"Hey, man, you like those boxes?" I asked.

"I suppose," I think he said.

"Presents for my folks. I made them."

He looked at me with those dismal eyes of his. "You did?" he asked.

"Yeah. Hard to do, though," I replied.

"I couldn't do it," he told me, like it was some fault of his.

"I made them in school," I said, so he wouldn't think I didn't have help.

He walked off, looking back over his shoulder at the boxes—not me—as he went to stuff his face with grub.

A couple of days later, about nine in the morning, Danny called me up. He said he wanted to see me about something. "Right away," he murmured. "It's important."

"Sure, fine," I said, not because I really wanted to talk to him, but I have to admit, I was curious. He rarely called me.

Then he said, "Has to be when your folks aren't around."

"How come?"

He hesitated. "Just does."

My folks both work—and it was still Christmas vacation for me—so that was easy. "You can come over now, if you want," I told him.

"Okay," he said. "I'll be there soon." Then he added, "You still have those boxes?"

"What boxes?"

"The ones you made."

"Still on display," I told him.

He grunted, then said, "See you." He hung up, loudly, like he'd dropped the phone rather than hung up normal. Made me sorry I invited him over.

When he called I was still lounging about in my pajamas and one of those heavy terry cloth bathrobes with the baggy pockets. I was going to dress, but instead I kept sitting in the living room, wondering what it was all about. Then, just as I reminded myself to get some real clothes on, the doorbell rang and there was Danny.

The first thing he said to me when he walked in was, "Your folks home?"

"I told you, no."

He lumbered on past me and went into the living room, knocking into the tall plant my mother had in the hallway. After setting the plant right, I followed him.

He was sitting on the living room couch, slumped over. He looked more miserable than ever, chin resting on his hands, eyes staring at the low table in front of the couch. On the table was a gun.

The gun was a small shiny silver pistol with a white handgrip. On TV cop shows I think they call them Saturday night specials, but I had never seen an actual one before.

Talk about getting goose bumps. I nearly froze to death. Really freaked. "Oh, man . . ." was just about all I could say.

He was staring at the gun.

"Where'd . . . you get that?" I stammered.

"A guy I know."

"What guy?"

"Hangs around school."

Trying to lighten things up a bit, I said, "What else did he give you?"

At first he didn't say anything. Then he reached into his pocket, fished around, and drew out his balled-up hand. And held it out to me. In his palm lay six bullets. Their casings were silver, the bullet heads were dark.

"That gun real?" I said.

Danny grunted, which I took to be yes.

Really upset, I just stood there, trying to figure what this was all about. Truth is, with that dejected look on his face and that gun and bullets, I was scared.

"This guy—*why* did he give it to you?" I asked.

After a long moment Danny said, "To make fun of me."

"I don't get it."

"I think he sells drugs, or something. And there are always these guys who hang around with him."

"Do you?"

"Do what?"

"Hang with him?"

He shook his head. Then he said, "But I watch them. I don't know why. They're always laughing. Fooling around. Then this guy suddenly looked at me and called me over. And at first I didn't think he meant me, but he said yes. So I went over. And he says, 'What you looking at?' And I said, 'Nothing.' And he said, 'You look like one dead dog. I mean, you look like you're nothing.'

"And I didn't say anything because I know it's true, so I just stood there. Then he said, 'Why don't you just do the whole job?' And I said, 'What?' And he said, 'Yeah, finish it off. Do something useful. Go kill yourself.'"

When I heard that, the hairs on the back of my neck crawled. I just stared at Danny, feeling a trickle of sweat slide down my back.

"People think I'm nothing," he said, looking like he was going burst into tears.

"That's not true," I whispered.

"It is true," he said, as much to himself as to me. "I don't have any friends. I go to school, but I hate it. I don't do much of anything. But all the time, *inside*, I have this . . . this fear in me."

"Fear about what?"

"About being who I am. Nothing. It's just always there. Inside."

"You ever talk to your parents?"

"No."

"Why?"

"I think they feel they same way."

"But you're not . . . going to *do* it, are you?"

He stared at the gun and squeezed the bullets in his fist till his knuckles turned white. "Yeah," he mumbled. "I am."

"But . . . why?"

"People think I can't do anything. That I'm a coward. I . . . I want to show people I'm not."

"I don't think you should," I said.

"Why?"

"You could fix things. You could. And you're just doing what someone told you to do, not what you want to do. I mean, you should talk to your mother. Your father. How do you think they'd feel?"

Actually, what I wanted to do was jump forward and grab the gun, but I didn't think I could. He was bigger than me. Besides, I was scared about myself too. I had heard about people getting killed in struggles for guns.

Then I thought, maybe the gun isn't loaded. But, like he was reading my mind, he began to load the gun, pushing the bullets into its handle. I had missed my chance.

"I just don't think you . . . should do it," I stammered.

He kept loading the gun. "I'm not so sure I should either," he said. "That's why I came here."

"What do you mean?"

"Those boxes," he said. He looked across the room. There they were, the two boxes I'd made, sitting on the mantle. "Bring them over here," he said. His voice was getting stronger. "Come on," he almost shouted. "Do it!"

Jolted, I fetched the boxes, one at a time, and put them on the low table before him.

"Maybe I won't do it," he said, his voice quavering a little. "But I have to try."

"Danny, you're not thinking," I said, edging forward. "You're—"

"I want to do what I want!" That time he did shout. It made me jump back.

He opened the two boxes. Into one of them, he put the gun.

"What are you doing?" I whispered.

He closed the lids. "Okay," he said, "here's where you come in. Just mix up the boxes. Then I pick one box. If I pick the one that has the gun inside it, I do it."

"Danny . . . that's crazy."

He shook his head. "It'll prove something."

"What?"

"I told you. That I can do it. See, if there's something inside, I do it. If nothing, I don't."

"Danny, please," I cried. "It's really insane!"

He looked at me. There was something wild in his eyes. He meant what he said.

"I'm not going to do it," I said.

"Then I'll pick without you. And I'll know which box it's in. This way you can give me a fifty-fifty chance."

"I don't want any part of this," I said.

"Too late," was his reply.

"It's so wrong!" I shouted. Then I wheeled around. "I'm calling the police."

"You call and I'll do it before they get here."

That stopped me. "Danny!" I shouted. "Please!" I was crying now, not knowing what to do.

He reached for the boxes, flipping open the lid of the one in which the gun now sat.

"No, wait!" I said. "I'll do it. Only, you have to promise you won't do anything if you pick the empty one."

He became thoughtful. Then he said, "Yeah, I promise."

"You going to leave the room?" I asked.

He shook his head.

"Then how am I going to do it?"

"I'll shut my eyes and count to . . . fifteen."

"You might peek."

"I won't. You going to do it?"

I took a deep breath. "Yeah."

He shut the box lid.

"And you promise," I said, "if you pick the box with nothing inside, you won't . . . you know, kill yourself? Danny, this is stupid!" I shouted.

"You going to help or not?" he demanded. He had become almost fierce.

I licked my lips. "I guess. . . ."

"I want to do it now," he said.

I edged a little closer. "You going to count fast or slow?"

"Medium," he said.

"And you promise you won't look?"

He nodded.

I got close to the boxes. "Okay," I said, my voice hoarse from tension.

He shut his eyes.

"Can you see me?" I asked.

"No."

I had this sudden thought of grabbing the gun and running out of the house with it. But I was too scared of what he might do.

Then, even as I tried to think that through, he said, "One!"

I reached for the boxes.

"Two! You're not shuffling them," he cried out. "I can hear. Three."

I shuffled the boxes, loudly as I could. As I did I glanced up, wanting to make sure he really had his eyes closed. Fast as anything, I dropped the gun into my bathrobe pocket.

He kept counting, and it seemed that he, you know, counted a little slower at the end. Then he finally said, "Fifteen." He opened his eyes and stared at the boxes. They were really identical. I mean you really couldn't tell one from the other, and of course, you couldn't see into them. I could see him swallowing, and that place over his jaw, near his ear, was fluttering.

"Please, Danny," I said, stepping back toward the doorway and praying like mad that he wouldn't see what I'd done. "Please, don't even choose."

For a while he just stared at the boxes. Never

looked at me. Not once. Then, with his hands shaking so hard I could see it, he reached forward. First he moved toward one box, stopped, and turned to the other. Then he swallowed hard, licked his lips, and, like, squirmed about on the couch. I was feeling sick. *Don't catch on,* I was saying to myself. *Don't catch on.*

Finally — and it looked like he had to force himself — he placed his hands — with a clunk — on one of the boxes.

I could hear — and see — his breathing as he drew the box toward him. Not that he opened it right away. He just sat there, his hands on the box, eyes closed. Tears were running down his cheeks.

He lifted his hands slightly and, using his thumbs, lifted the box lid. His eyes were still closed. Then he opened them.

"Empty!" he cried. Oh, man, it was one huge shout of relief. Then he threw himself back against the couch and started to cry.

I watched him. Would he or would he not check

the other box? I decided I had to take the chance. I went out into the hall to the phone and called my father. "What's up?" he asked.

"It's Danny," I said. "Get here quick. And you'd better call one of his parents too."

My dad did get there quick, and when I told him what happened he took over, starting by putting his arms around Danny, who was still crying. Then Danny's mother came. And there were a lot of tears, and I kept hearing Danny say, "I didn't want to do it."

After a while Danny and his mother went home. I was standing there, still in my bathrobe, looking at my father. He was sitting in his easy chair, lost in his own thoughts. He suddenly looked up. "Do you think he would have killed himself if he had opened the other box?"

"No," I said.

Puzzled, he looked at me. "What makes you so sure?"

I went over to the other — still closed — box and

flipped open the lid. Of course it was empty too.

"I don't get it," he said, obviously baffled.

I pulled the pistol out of my bathrobe pocket and handed it to him. "When he had his eyes closed," I explained, "I made sure both boxes had nothing inside."

My dad stared at me.

I said, "Nothing inside the box but his life. Good thing he couldn't see that."

FoRTUNE COOKIE

Okay, you want my side of the story. Hey, no problem. It begins cool. But it ends . . . well . . . I have to tell you.

See, my parents had been divorced for about eight months. Then along comes my first birthday since that captivating event occurred. Like, I figure, this has to be something special. I'm about to become a teenager. Way killer.

When my folks got divorced it was supposed to be a joint custody thing. But as far as I could figure out, my father thought that "joint custody" meant that he could live in his own joint, while my mom could take care of the custody part. I was living with my mom along with my younger sister. Course now and again Dad was willing to see us—when it fit his schedule. So, since he wasn't living that far away, I saw him once in a while.

When I did see him we'd do a movie or dinner, maybe both. With him you never knew. I even spent a couple of weekends with him—and his girlfriend, whose name is Louise. I call her Lulu. Killer boring. Most of the time I watched TV. Copped some of Lulu's cigs. Worked on my addiction. She didn't care. I mean she didn't want to be my mother. Sister, maybe. Friend. Who knew? Not me.

Anyway, for some reason that I never figured out, my father always called me on Tuesday nights. I mean, I know *why* he called me, but I don't know his reasons for picking Tuesdays. As far as days go, Tuesday is what? Like, not exactly ripe. Know what I'm saying? On Thursdays he called my little sister.

So there it was, my birthday coming up and he calls me the last Tuesday before it happens. Three-day warning.

" . . . okay, pal," he said, after he asked me official father questions like, "How are you doing? How is school? See anything good on TV? Did you see the Cowboys game?" Once we got this sitcom dad talk out of the way, he said, "Listen here, pal, your thirteenth birthday is coming up. That's a big one. I'd really like to get you something nice. So what would you like? How about you suggesting something?"

"Anything?" I said. You know, checking, 'cause my dad is big on promises, small on delivery.

"Well, you know," he said, sort of backing off and blowing off black murk like a squid, "anything within reason."

"Yeah," I said, "I've been thinking." Which was true. I'd been working on what it meant to have my first birthday with my parents split and all that. I mean, birthdays are important. I know, there must be tons of people — millions — born on the same day, but you don't know that. You think it's your own day. Know what I'm saying? The day belongs to you. It's like writing your own fortune cookie. Cool.

So I said to him, "I'd like to go out to dinner with you —"

"Hey, great. Love it. You're on."

"Yeah, just you, me . . . and mom."

For a moment he didn't say anything. I had blind-sided him. Anyway, he took the hit and breathed. He does that — breathing — normally, I know, but when he's uptight, you *hear* it, like a smoker running the two hundred right after dinner. Sure enough, he says, "Your *mom*?"

"Yeah, you know," I said. "The one you were married to for fifteen years. Remember her? Brown hair. About five six, with hazel eyes, dumpy figure, who is supposed to get regular child-support checks —"

"Parker . . . ," he said, "I don't need your sarcasm."

"I wasn't being sarcastic," I said. "But isn't my idea within reason?" I asked. "Having a birthday dinner with my mom and my dad doesn't seem to be such a big deal to me."

Of course I was lying. It was a big deal. I knew it. He knew it. Thing was, I knew he wouldn't *say* it. Like, I love putting my parents on the edge. You know, the absolute edge. It forces them to be themselves. Makes 'em squirm. For real. And best of all, I can watch.

He says, "I don't know. . . . Your mother and I have sort of given up talking these days. When I need to know something, I speak to . . . uh . . ." He stumbled for words.

"Me?" I suggested. "And Sarah. On Thursdays. But what about the dog? You know, Big Foot misses you. In fact, he misses you most of all. Lately it's been so bad he's been asking about his dog-support checks. Really, Dad, you should call him too. Maybe give him Sunday."

"Back off, Parker. Back off."

"Don't worry," I said, "I'm not asking you and Mom to renew your sacred vows and get married again. I just—"

"Okay. Okay," he cut in. "You ask her. See what she says. Then get back to me."

"Cool."

"You know my beeper number."

"Right," I said. "And you know mine, 666."

I slammed down the phone, lay back on my bed, and tried to think out my next step. Because the next step was asking my ma.

My ma works as a legal assistant at some stock-brokers' place downtown. She puts in long days for little pay and then comes home to us all beat up. We beat her up some more.

After school we have a baby-sitter. Me, at my age, with a baby-sitter! These baby-sitters are usually college girls—excuse me, young women—and they don't stay very long, mostly because I give them a hard time and then they quit. Not that they ever tell my ma that I am the cause. Since they tend to like her they usually say something about a lot of schoolwork. No way.

Like, with one of them—her name was Dora— one day I said, "Hey, cool, you have a mustache. Does it tickle the guys you kiss?" Next day, she was out of there. But, hey, I'm honest.

Anyway, I made my way to Mom's room. She wasn't there. I went to my sister's cave. I mean, it is a room, but Sarah keeps it dark, and she never picks up her stuff from the floor. So it's like a cave, or better yet, an abandoned cave, a cave that's about to collapse. I think she's hiding. But then she's only nine.

She was there, and so was my mother. My mother was helping her do homework. My ma's not supposed to do that, but Sarah is a whiner, and my ma gives in. If I whine, she gets sore. Look, I'm just telling you the way it is.

"Hey, Mommy . . . ," I called.

"Just a minute," she said. "I'm working with Sarah."

As if I hadn't noticed that for myself. I mean, the way I see it is, one of the basic jobs parents have is to tell you what you already know. Know what I'm saying? Echo machines.

Anyway, I said, "Something incredibly important came up that I need to talk to you about. It's so awesome urgent it'll change the course of my life forever. But it can wait." I left the room, making sure my baseball cap was on backward. It bugs her.

By the time my mother came into my room it was about nine-thirty, and I was stretched out on my bed doing nothing but listening to some loud music, which is the only way to go. Otherwise you think too much.

People always say kids like me don't think enough. But I'll tell you, actually, we think too much. We just don't let on.

Well, she stood by the door, leaning on the frame. I could see she was tired. And I knew she wasn't going to be thrilled by my birthday idea, but a teenager has to do what he's got to do. Hey, we're practicing to be adults.

"You said you had something important . . . ," she said. From the look on her face, I could tell she didn't really believe me, but was prepared to listen to me like a good ma should. And my ma is good. I know that because she's always telling me.

"Yeah, right, it's about my birthday. . . ."

Her face softened. "Thirteen years old. Would you like to have some friends over? Do something special?"

"I want an arm tattoo of a busty nude lady fighting a python caught between her legs."

"No."

"I want to have my left nipple pierced with a gold chain that attaches to my right nostril."

"No."

"Third time lucky. I want to go out for dinner."

"Well, sure . . . though I have a small gift already. But if it's not too pricy a place."

"No, I mean, I want to go out to dinner with you and Dad."

Same as with my father, she didn't say anything for a bit. And, like I figured, it was obvious she wasn't very happy about my suggestion. I mean, there was this really pained look on her face, so painful, I admit, I almost lost my nerve. But since I'd made a vow with myself to really do this thing I kept on.

"Why?" she said.

"Hey, I just thought it would be cool," I said in my best wicked way. "I mean, you are my parents. Both of you. I mean, at least that's what we learned in bio class. And it is *my* birthday. It's what I want."

"Is this your idea or his?"

"Mine."

"I gather you've spoken to him about it."

"Yeah."

"What did he say?"

"He said it was a nasty idea."

"Parker, for once tell me straight: Does he really *want* to do this?"

"He got panicky. But I guess you don't want to do it either, right?"

She thought for a moment, then said, "To be honest, I don't."

"Well, to be honest myself, I like it. I think he said he'd do it if you would. It's a democracy. Majority rules."

"Families are not governments," she said, grim faced. "What about your sister?"

"No way. She'll cry. Just you, Dad, and me. The mature ones."

"I'll think about it," she said, and wheeled around and left the room.

So then I called my dad back. "Hey, Dad," I said, "Ma thinks having the birthday dinner with just the three of us is a gross idea. My guess is that she's so disgusted with your behavior, she can't see sitting down with you even for an hour."

"Parker . . . show some respect."

"You wanted a report."

"Well . . ."

"My guess is that if she says no, you'll say yes, because that way you get to put her down. Am I right?" He grunted. But he swallowed the bait.

"If the three of us having dinner is what you want . . ."

There it was. I had him on the line. I mean, who's going to control my life, me or them?

I went back to my mother. She was in bed, reading some legal brief. I sat on the edge of the bed.

"Well, what do you think?" I said.

She looked over her papers at me. "About what?"

"Dinner. You. Me. Dad."

"I hate it."

"Why?"

She thought a minute, trying to find a way not to say what she really felt. She said, "Because there is so much bad feeling. I want your birthday to be a happy time. What you're suggesting will be an unpleasant evening."

"Gee," I said, "I always thought you were the kind of mother who loved her kids so much that she could swallow her pain and pride and do what was best for them, not herself."

She glared at me. "Parker, where do you get this stuff?"

"A book at the library called *A Kids' Guide to Divorce.*" I got off the bed. "But if you want to be the uncompromising parent . . ."

"Parker," she cried, "I love you enough to say that there are times I hate you. You are very manipulative."

I grinned. The lady understood. So I said, "Hey, you noticed. That means yes, you'll do it, right?"

"Right," she said, and pretended to go back to her papers.

Now, I suppose you'd like to know why I wanted to do this. That's cool. I mean, I know that my parents

come to dislike each other. Like,
divorced, they were into all these
ing, not talking to each other, door
, blah, blah. Like, there was so much
em̲ ̲ ̲ ̲ ̲ ̲needed a spoon, no, a shovel, to heave
it. Bummer. Like, suffocating. I mean, man, it was a
relief when they sat us down and informed us that
they were going to split. Well, sure, Sarah had a knot-
ted spaghetti fit, cried and all that junk. As for me, I
already knew the world was round, if you know what
I'm saying.

But the thing is, I was curious. I mean some time
had gone by, and I just wanted to see how they would
act with each other. Yeah, call me odd. I mean, I'm one
of those people who likes to watch people. And the
way I see it, is there anything better than watching
your own parents squirm?

Okay. Before I know it, it's October the twelfth. My
birthday.

I'll set the scene. It's a kind of gray, blustery

evening. Likelihood of rain. My sister is whining. Why can't *she* go? I tell her it's because she isn't tall enough, that the restaurant we're going to doesn't have kiddy cushions. She walks off in a huff and slams the door to her cave. Fine. Whatever it takes. Mission accomplished.

Baby-sitter for Sarah arrives. My ma and I go out. She insisted she would drive: pick my dad up and take us to the restaurant.

"Why?"

"Your father is a control freak."

"Hey, the politicians say you're not doing your parent job unless you control your kids."

"Parker, I hate this."

"Mommy dear, it's my birthday."

We got into the car and drove to my father's apartment. As we got close, she said, "Is his girlfriend joining us?"

"Lulu?"

She winced. "Her name is Louise."

"Lulu isn't old enough to go out at night. She'll stay home with her baby-sitter too."

My mother looked at me. "You can be very cruel."

"What you call cruel I call honest."

"I dread this," she admitted.

I gave her a thumbs up. "Bigtime killer event."

My father was waiting on the curb. He was in a suit and tie. My mother was in her office uniform. I had baggy pants, a torn Grateful Dead T-shirt, and my cap on backward. So we all had our proper trick-or-treat costumes.

He climbed into the back seat. "Hi," he said.

"Hello, Peter," my mother said.

Ignoring her, my father said, "Happy birthday, Parker," to me.

"Never happier," I said.

My mother drove off, stone-faced. I felt my sympathy rising, but I pushed it down, reminding myself that I had to see things through.

"Ah," my father said, trying to sound casual, "where are we going?"

"Ming's Golden Dragon," I said.

"Oh, very nice," he said. "I enjoy Chinese."

"Lucky for you there are a lot of them," I said.

"Parker . . . ," my mother warned.

We drove along without anyone saying anything. I hate silence. All you hear is yourself. So I leaned forward and flipped on the radio. The music was loud, but I made it louder. "Bleeding Ingrown Toenails," I announced.

"I beg your pardon?" my mother said.

"Name of my favorite band," I explained.

"Turn it down," she said.

"Betty," my father says, "it's his birthday." A cheap shot.

There was no more talk until we got to the restaurant. It was a fairly big place—my family used to go there about once a month B.D.—Before Divorce. It has round tables in the center, booths along the sides. On the walls are plastic dragons. On each table are fake flowers and a bottle of soy sauce.

"How many, please?" the dude at the door asked.

"Three," my father said.

"Table or booth?"

"Table," I said. "Middle of the room."

My mother shot me a dirty look, but it was too late. The host led us to a table right in the middle of the place. The dead center. Cool. Eye of the storm. Loved it.

We sat down. Menus were brought. No one had said much of anything. My parents looked at the menus while I looked at my father and my mother, who were spending most of the time not looking at each other. I mean, how do you handle it when the two most important people in your life hate each other? Take 'em to dinner.

"It's your birthday," my father finally said to me. "You choose. I'll pay."

"It's about time," I said.

"We'll share," my mother insisted.

"And we all share the food, right?" I said.

"Fine with me," my mother said.

Instead of looking at the menu, I said to my father, "Well, Dad, how's Lulu? She going to finish high school this year?"

He scowled. "Louise is fine, thank you. And she does not go to high school."

"Keeping her dumb, eh?"

His face turned red. I heard his breathing. "She spends most of her time working."

"Right. Dental hygienist. Cool. Hey, man, smile. Your teeth *are* looking better."

"Parker . . . ," my mother growled.

The waiter approached, hunched over in a slight bow, order pad in hand.

"Ready to order, please?" he asked. Which means, "Move it, dudes!"

I picked up the menu, which I hadn't really looked at yet. I rattled off, "For appetizers, we'll have the Pu

Pu Platter, Shark Fin Soup, then main course, Pork Moo Shi and Slippery Chicken."

"Excellent choices," the waiter said, which he probably said to anyone who ordered anything. Off he bowed.

There was a moment of silence. "Hope you like the Slippery Chicken," I said to my dad. "I ordered that for you." I turned to my mom. "Shark Fin Soup for you."

"And for yourself?" she asked between clenched teeth.

"Pu Pu Platter."

We went back to silence.

"Did you tell Dad about Charles Rosterman the Third?" I suddenly said to my mother.

Her face turned pink.

My father looked up. He wasn't going to ask.

I explained it to him: "Your former wife and the Third — that's what I call him — have been dating. He's a broker where she works. Specializes in hog futures."

"That's nice."

"He's incredibly rich, but, guess what."

"What?"

"He's been through three marriages. Which as I read it means he doesn't know much about women, but when it comes to hogs, hey, awesome."

My mother, getting angrier by the minute, leaned forward. "Exactly what are you trying to do?" she asked me.

"Embarrass everybody."

"You're succeeding. What about yourself?"

"Hey, cool," I said. "Take a shot."

She held off since the waiter came to give us the Pu Pu Platter. When he left, she said, "Parker, why can't you act your age?"

"Biological, emotional, or mental?" I asked.

My father said, "I was hoping this would be nice."

"Why?" I asked him.

"Because you asked for it."

"Look," I said, "the way I see it, you two have me,

right? Maybe you didn't plan to. Hey, mistakes happen. You could have had an abortion, but you didn't. So, here I am. Pro-life exhibit A. Oh, yeah, and Sarah. Ditto. But then, after a while, you decided you didn't like each other, and you split. Not that you asked us. But, hey, it's none of our business. Right? Then you," I said to my father, "forget that you're supposed to buy food for us. You let Mom take care of all that little stuff. And you," I said to my mother, "are so angry, tired, and trapped, you can't see straight anymore and you blame us for being needy.

"Now, what I called this little meeting for is to raise the question, what am I supposed to do about you two?"

There was some stony silence. In the middle of it the soup was served. My parents just sat there, white faced, staring in front of them. Not at me, not at each other.

I said, "Anyone want the rest of this Pu Pu? It's awesome."

It was my mother who spoke up. "Parker, I think you have no concern other than for yourself."

"That's cool," I said. "Who else is going to have concern for me?"

"What about other people?" she asked. "Me? Or your sister?"

My father leaned over the table and clasped his hands. "Did your mother put you up to this?"

"Nope. I did. And one of these days you're going to have to accept the fact that Mom doesn't work for the CIA, FBI, or IRS, that she doesn't spend all her time plotting to kneecap you. You know what she wants?"

"What?"

"Child-support checks. So she can get on with her life. You didn't divorce her. You put her in a box."

He slapped his hand on the table so hard it made the teacups rattle. Everybody in the restaurant looked around.

I grinned and said, "Hey, dude, I chose a middle table so everybody could watch what you do."

He looked me hard in the eyes and murmured, "You bastard. . . ."

"Hey, you ought to know."

"Parker . . ." I heard my mother warn.

My father got up from the table, took two steps away, then came back and sat down.

The waiter served the Pork Moo Shi and Slippery Chicken.

We ate. No one spoke. My stomach was in such knots I thought I would throw up. But I kept going.

"Okay, Dad," I said, "what's with the child support? It's a bummer you're not paying."

He said, "That is an issue that I will discuss only with your mother."

I said, "You know what I'm going to do?"

"No."

"If my mother ever gets married again, I'm going to leave her and move in with you and Lulu. For revenge. Don't say I didn't warn you."

He looked grim. All he said, though, was, "Fine."

I turned to my ma. "Or I might stay with you and the Third, if you promise not to blame Dad for all the misery in your life."

She scowled at me.

"Hey, Dad, guess what Mom got me for a birthday present?"

"I don't know."

"Two tickets to a Balding Sweethearts concert."

"That's nice."

"What did you get me?"

He frowned. "I told you you could have asked for something reasonable. I would have given you money but I thought that would be tacky. Then you said you wanted this dinner. But if you want more I'll come up with something."

"Hey, you never said anything about money," I said. "I don't think money's tacky. I would have taken it. Like, we need it."

"Excuse me," my mother said, and she threw her napkin on the table, got up, and walked to the ladies' room. I think she didn't want to cry in public.

I grabbed hold of my chair. It was like I was going ninety-seven miles an hour and I was about to fall out of the driver's seat. For a sec I shut my eyes. When I opened them I realized my father was staring at me, furious.

"Parker," he barked, "what in God's name are you trying to do?"

"Embarrass you."

"Why?"

"You're my very own deadbeat dad."

He shoved himself back in his chair. "Your mother did put you up to this, didn't she?"

"Hey, like, I've got my own brain, dude."

He reached into his jacket, pulled out a wallet, took out a twenty-dollar bill, and threw it on the table. "Tell your mother I had an important meeting."

With that he got up and walked out of the restaurant.

I watched him go. It was the worst moment. I mean I was alone then, except this time it was my doing. I hardly knew what to scream at him: "Stay away!" or

"Come back!" Then I began to wonder if either of them would come back. I felt sick.

But right on cue — the way God should do it — the waiter deposited the fortune cookies. I stared at them for a long time. I love fate. It means I don't have to do anything.

My mother returned. She had been crying. "Where's your father?"

"He said to tell you he had an important meeting. Which reminds me, my birthday fortune has arrived. Are you ready for the truth?" I picked the thing up.

Looking like she was fighting back tears, she said, "Let's go home."

"Wait!" I shouted. "Fate speaks to us in mysterious ways. To ignore it is to bring doom!"

"Come on!"

I put the fortune cookie in my pocket.

Mom and I drove back home. There was silence at first. Then she said, "Did you achieve what you wanted?"

"I don't know."

"What did you want to happen?"

"Don't know that either."

She said, "You love your father a lot, don't you?"

That caught me by surprise. Which I hate. But as I said, I'm honest. So, after a while, I said, "Yeah."

"Why?"

"Wish I knew."

She said nothing. Exhausted, I just stared at the passing headlights. They reminded me of the spears of jousting knights. Everybody getting killed. But no one stopped moving. Zombie traffic.

"What about me?" she finally said, her voice trembling, almost whispering. "What are your feelings?"

"Like, I love you too."

"That's just words," she said.

"You're right."

"Well . . . then?"

I took a deep breath. "For you I've got something better than love."

"What's that?"

"I . . . trust you."

"Why?"

"You'll never hurt me."

"Thank you."

"But . . ."

"But, what?"

I said, "That means I'll hurt you."

"Why?"

"'Cause, like I said, you'll never hurt me back."

She reached out, touched my hand, but we didn't talk for the rest of the ride.

The rain started to come down, making the tar roads look like they were coated with cheap silver.

It was only when I got to bed, shut the door tight, turned on the music loud, that I took out the fortune cookie and cracked it open. The little yellow paper slip read: "Many people will love you."

That's when I began to cry. But, hey, no one could see me. Killer.